Rainbows in the Desert and Other Stories

Rainbows in the Desert
and Other Stories

Archna Pant

LiFi Publications Pvt. Ltd.
New Delhi

Published by:
LiFi Publications Pvt. Ltd.
211, 2nd Floor, Gagandeep
12, Rajendra Place, New Delhi–110 008, India
Phone : (011) 2574 1000
E-mail : info@lifipublications.com
Web : www.lifipublications.com

ISBN 13: 978-93-82536-14-7 ISBN 10: 93-82536-14-0

First published in 2014

Cataloging in Publication Data—DK
[Courtesy: D.K. Agencies (P) Ltd. <docinfo@dkagencies.com>]

Pant, Archna, 1959–
Rainbows in the desert and other stories / Archna Pant.
p. cm.
Short stories.
ISBN 9789382536147

1. Emotions--Fiction. 2. Interpersonal relations--Fiction.
3. Short stories, Indic (English). I. Title.

DDC 823.92 23

Printed in India by D.K. Fine Art Press (P) Ltd., Delhi–52

To my mother Smt. Tara Pande, who's no more:
for all those stories in the dark of the night
and the warmth of her snuggle.

My father Sri Laxmi Kant Pande:
for passing on to me the joy of the written word.

And Gurumai Shanthamma:
without whom none of this would have been possible.

Contents

Preface

My romance with stories started as a child, when snuggling into my mother's warmth in the dark bliss of the night I'd listen to her stories with bated breath. They were stories that could never lull me to sleep but made me come alive in a million ways.

Across the years, I sought them over and over again in fairy tales, folklores, text books, anywhere and everywhere. I came to realise that every face, every life has a story behind it. I've been lucky enough to have met exceptional human beings from the humblest and most ordinary stations of life. These encounters in my day to day life have revealed to me the glory of the human spirit, its tenacity to face adversities and yet keep going, preserving the joy and beauty of life intact.

These stories needed to be told, to be penned down for others to reaffirm their faith in humanity's strength and grandeur. These are not simply a cluster of seven stories written randomly on a whim. They have a deep underlying connection with the will that lies buried in the human heart; the will that may be tormented but refuses to get crushed.

My stories deal with ordinary people recognisable in that they are likely to cross our path or are like people already known to us; and vulnerable to the manipulations of other people, because in themselves they have a core of goodness that others well know how to exploit. In this sense even my stories that end happily have a tragic note in them.

This might make it seem that the stories are divided, in characterisation, between black and white but it isn't that simple because the villains are seemingly unaware that they are villainous, yet cruel beyond measure. This ominous fixity of their selfishness and machinations leads to stories that remind us that the world is a sad place, but lit up by occasional flashes of things turning out right despite the existence of such blots on mankind's conscience.

I detail my stories a lot, but more than my detailing and my few descriptions of places and nature, what one is finally left with to cherish, I hope, are the human and humane relationships I portray in their complex warp and weft and that too in intricate networks among different ages, genders and generations.

I am a humanist and my stories speak of the emotionally and economically underprivileged, and of women suppressed and denied their rights from generations countless. But everywhere my mayhap deep, sober and psychological insights on life are, I feel, worth perusing. No story in this collection is a light read and each has its own plus points....

The stories in the collection are:

Rainbows in the Desert: An innocent lively girl child is married off to a much older man. But she manages to create rainbows even in the desert.

Lessons of Life: An orphaned boy craving for love and home leaves his beautiful valley to chase an elusive dream.

Lucknow Mail: A self willed daughter of a professor resents her father's decision of inviting his poor research scholar to live with them. Yet...

Mirages of the Heart: An old woman who's generous enough to allow all her relatives to exploit her, lovingly forgives her son his apathetic behaviour in the past...

Reasons of the Heart: A wilful, old lady, living alone, takes in an equally headstrong young man as a tenant. Sparks fly!

Justice for Janaki: An ayah of a college is regularly beaten and finally murdered by her husband. Do they, she and her daughter find justice finally?

Wind beneath the Wings: A young girl who studied management dreams of empowerment, liberation and love. Will her dreams turn sour?

These are all stories of people who struggle everyday to live with dignity and honour, to claim their space of land and sky, to create golden tomorrows for those who shall inherit this earth afterwards.

My stories reflect life the way it is, in the urban and rural milieu of India, watching it through the prism of human emotions and complexities, studying the layers of human emotions and interpersonal relationships.

I have been influenced by writers like Premchand, O Henry and Chekhov who deal with life as it is, in the direct and the raw, in their stories. Their portrayal of human nature, their insight into la condition humaine and love for humanity, is what has impressed and influenced me most about their writings. It has helped me to veer away from taking the easy route in my own of giving to the readers shallow writing and instead to try for their kind of balanced, simple and profound art. If I have succeeded even in a small measure, in this my first collection of short stories, it is a big victory for me. The social and cultural and historical milieu in my stories is what I know of and this too shows their realist influence on my writing.

My stories spring from my own experiences in life, so they are very feminine in thought and content. I have endeavoured into a genre of writing where in a few hundred words a world can be spoken of, a world can be created. I hope you enter my world fully and enjoy it as much as I did in offering all of it to you, with all of my heart.

Archna Pant

Acknowledgement

We are never alone in our journey. There are hands that pat us on our back, faces that smile at us, voices that urge us on, hearts that offer their warmth and support generously and there are souls like shining stars who light up our path in the darkest of nights.

This book too would not have been possible without those countless people who shared their stories with me directly-indirectly, who allowed me a peep into the deepest recesses of their minds and hearts, who revealed to me their trials, tribulations, dreams, hopes and faith.

I salute their courage, strength and the glory of their spirit.

My first bow of gratitude to my Guru Maa. To my parents who passed on to me their love for humanity and the written word. My heartfelt obeisance to my other set of parents – Ijaji for your irrepressible love for life and for having shared those thousand stories locked away in your heart. Bauji for your infinite goodness and compassion.

Thanks to all my teachers and friends of St. Angela Sophia H.S. School for enjoying my writing even back then and for making me believe in myself. Thanks also to Maharani College, Jaipur and R.A. Podar Institute of Management, University Of Jaipur, for honing my skills along the way. Thank you Mr. P.S. Shetty and Mr. R.K. Caprihan for teaching me all about the corporate world.

I wish to thank each and everyone at LiFi publications for their support and professionalism.

A most special word of thanks for my dearest friend Dr. Bina Biswas, a sensitive and renowned author herself, who inspires me everyday with her creativity and work ethics, as also for her amazing editorial inputs. This book would not have been possible without her faith in me.

Deeply obliged to my role model the iconic Sathya Saran (Ex Editor Femina and best selling Author) for her encouragement and guidance from time to time as also to Sumana Roy, Lecturer, Poet and Author for her kindness and support.

My reverence and gratitude to Dr. M.C. Joshi, retd. Prof. of English, Jodhpur University for his vision, insight and guidance.

Thanks and regards to my friend Dr. A.V. Koshy a truly great poet and author (who the world shall remember in times to come) for hanging on to his faith in my writing as also for teaching me the finer nuances of this craft.

Thanks to my soul sisters Dr. Nidhi Tandon, Tulika Sharma and to Mrs. Priti J Purohit who were the most enthusiastic readers and critics for each story.

A warm hug and 'I'm blessed to have a sister like you.' To Shobha Pande.

Love and thanks to my support system Meera Joshi, Dinesh Joshi, Lata Pant, Pramod Pant, Kanchan Joshi, Dinesh Joshi, Meeru Pant, Anupama Pant, Aditi Joshi, Nidhi Pant, Narayan Sharma, Asha Sharma, Dr. Shubhra Sharma and to all my online friends.

Col H.V. Pant and Anita 'Together we'll win.'

A million thanks.

To you, my readers, for that leap of faith in picking up the book of a debut author.

And over and above all, to the reason for all rainbows in my life, my husband Mr. Harish Pant who dreamt my dreams for me and gave me his unconditional support (Thank you for being the wind beneath my wings Hari!) as also to my son Anurag Pant who is my daily reminder of all that is beautiful and good in this world. (God bless!)

Love,
Archna Pant

1

Rainbows in the Desert

It was just nine in the morning and I could already feel all the muscles and tissues of my body protesting against their violation. It had been a hectic morning. Rising up at five to start the online motor and the booster pump, then going straight to the kitchen as if on an auto pilot; my hands busy juggling ten odd chores simultaneously. Tea for Vinay with his Marie biscuits, milk for Nandini with a half boiled egg, tiffin to be packed just so, water in the flask, clothes laid out, shoes polished, followed by breakfast for Vinay, lunch cooked for his office while he took his bath, vegetables bought from the vendor who came just then, milk boiled, curd set for the day and dishes washed. So by nine when all had left and the house fell silent like an empty classroom; I sat down finally with my first steaming cup of tea. And it was then that I could feel every muscle in my body groan in protest and fatigue.

It had been a month since Vinay had taken up this new assignment in Lucknow. A month of unrelenting physical labour for me, with all the unpacking, arranging, organising of the new establishment; while performing all the household chores singlehandedly in absence of any help. A month of hard backbreaking routine (along with the additional jobs of managing Nandini's mid-term admission in the new school, buying new set of books, getting her uniforms stitched) and I could feel my nerves frayed to the point of tears. I had sounded off my desperation to a couple of acquaintances and neighbours hoping that someone would be able to scout out a genie for me but all that I had received so far were just blank assurances.

Lost in this reverie I nearly missed the doorbell chime not once but twice. Startled out of my stupor the third time, I opened the door to find Rama my neighbour standing with a victorious twinkle in her eyes and a fairly young, slender, dusky woman of medium height, dark *kohl* lined eyes dominating her face, fidgeting shyly with her *pallu*; hiding behind her. She was in a faded clean sari, darned at several places and a blouse which was far too loose and mismatched. However I observed that her long thick plait hanging behind reaching her hips was lustrous enough to make any woman envy her.

Rama who's known for her informal demeanour along with her heart of gold had already plonked herself on the couch and was merrily twittering away about how her heart was so moved by my predicament, about how a woman's lot is the worst on this earth, how finding someone honest and hard working was more difficult than finding a rainbow in the desert and how she remembered Malati right in the middle of her bath (which is where all her thoughts were unleashed). She could create such a lively picture with words that one actually shuddered at the idea of having her running out of her bath, screaming, "Eureka! Eureka! I've found her."

Rama then launched a nonstop monologue on Malati. How she had first noticed Malati while going around a slum settlement as a volunteer of an NGO, to pick up children for free primary education. She claimed to have noticed Malati instantly because of that something which set her apart from the rest of them all – her neatness, her refined behaviour, her soft melodious voice.

Soon after when her sister needed a maid desperately, Rama found herself going back again to that dwelling and with the help of her natural spontaneous warmth, managed to bring Malati out from the walls of her cloistered life into a new world of people and profession.

Over the time with word of the mouth, Malati was able to secure a few more part time jobs. Slowly and steadily a woman who had never walked out of her dwellings learnt to face the world and its complexities with an ease she never knew she possessed.

Destiny plays its own chess with human lives. Just as we had come to Lucknow Rama's sister left for Delhi on transfer and Malati needed to pick up yet another job. This was precisely when Rama had that flash of divine enlightenment while having her bath.

And this was precisely how Malati quietly walked into my life at 9 a.m. one fine morning. A shy and timid soul, she'd be at my doorstep everyday sharp 7.30 a.m. Leaving her worn out slippers outside, she'd tip toe into my seemingly endless day with the ease and grace of a ballet dancer. Her quietude, her spontaneous calm and peace radiated into my life and filled me up with a serenity I'd never known before.

It was then I realised that age has nothing to do with the years we have lived, with the number of times our bodies have perambulated the temple of six seasons, and it has nothing to do with the wear and tear of our cells. Age happens to us every time we face the autumns of our life with no possibilities of summers, just the chill of the winter looming ahead, the skies grey and our trees bereft of leaves; but we still carry our hopes like the dormant seeds deep inside the soil and we are still able to sing the songs of spring.

Age happens to us when like a village belle with all the earthen pots of trials, tribulations, miseries and pain balanced precariously on our head; we're still able to sway gracefully to the rhythm of life around us, still able to smile and wink at destiny and keep our dreams intact.

Age happens to us when nothing fazes us anymore, when we can look straight into the eyes of life and hold her gaze without anticipation or fear, when neither loss nor tragedy, neither disappointment nor devastation can make us bat an eyelid.

Thus for her twenty nine years to my thirty five, Malati was far ahead of me in age and maturity. Her repose was just the right foil for my anxious temperament. As the days went by I found that not only she was sincere and hard working but that for her commitments ran deep and that she was a person of impeccable grit and character. Rama had already informed me that she was quite unlike other maids. Very reserved, reticent, she never talked about herself, never gossiped, nor asked for any favours.

But strange as the ways of life are, over the months, I found her responding to me diffidently but surely. Initially it was me doing all the conversation, while she would communicate through a smile, a nod, or at the most by the movement of her eyes. But as the time passed and our association deepened, she understood my levels of empathy and commitment too. This realisation broke down all her walls of reserve and aloofness and cemented a bond which was deeper than any other I'd ever experienced.

Unknowingly she made herself indispensible to me. There was a quintessential mother in her who seemed to take over all my insecurities, restlessness and my simple ignorance behind the I-know-it-all exterior. I on my part enjoyed every bit of the emotional pampering her subtle gestures offered. She could handle Nandini more lovingly and firmly than I ever could and to my extreme surprise my little smart aleck could sense the undercurrent of authority with the same acuteness with which a headstrong filly knows the master's hand. This authority instead of making her resentful created a strong bond of respect and love for my saviour angel.

As the association grew and as grew our mutual trust and faith in each other; I got to learn more and more about this dusky, shy mystery woman in my life. She was born in Dausa, a small village in between Jaipur and Bharatpur in Rajasthan. It was a childhood of sheer fun and bliss. She could recall every tiny detail so vividly and picturesquely that I would listen to her with unabated fascination. Her words would paint the lush green *bajra* and wheat fields and the gorgeous yellow carpet of mustard fields, rolled out as far as the eyes could see. She spun stories of Kawaraoji, the fort of Bargujars, Chand Baori the 100 ft deep well with 3500 steps on three sides and the Neelkanth Mahadev Mandir where she would run around with her friends all day long.

Her imageries were vibrantly colourful and bright, so much that when she described any part of her childhood, I could feel the colours dancing right in front of my eyes. Her recollections of sitting under a *Khejri* tree, secretly eating *ber* and *imli* with her best friend Muniya, of the group of girls going to school together (strangely for a village of Rajasthan, Dausa showed a lot of willingness, to educate its girls), the irresistible smell of Mango pickles and *parathas* during the tiffin time, the cold breeze in the night after the dry hot winds of the day, the simmering fire of the *sigri* and the *dal-baati-choorma* being cooked on it along with the spicy hot *kair-saangri*; all had a magical sense of immediacy which was truly admirable.

Life for them was like the transparent stole of sand, *Odhani*, which their earth wore. Theirs were elementary joys and simple sorrows.

Her mother a simple, docile woman, who like other woman of her land, was meant to be seen and not heard. She kept her head covered all the time and remained busy in the kitchen and the cow barn for most part of her day. She remembered her mother churning out rich white butter, homemade ghee and fresh buttermilk every afternoon. Her father worked in the fields and came home only for his meals and rest.

Malati loved her simple life but much more than anything, she loved to study. She loved books. She dreamt of being a teacher one day, who'd be able to mould the tender, young minds of tomorrow. Little did she know that life always keeps the last laugh for itself!

It was a bad summer that year, there were no rains and all the crops had dried up. Malati's father had taken a loan from the Mahajan and it was devastating to think of what would happen when the Mahajan would demand his money back at the end of the year. Her mother's jewellery too had been pawned off much earlier, so there was really nothing to fall back on. Malati was then studying in class tenth with two younger sisters and a brother. Their future too was a big question mark for their father now.

It was during this period of mental turbulence that Ramesh's family came to meet them with a marriage proposal for Ramesh; who was a widower more than twice the age of Malati. His wife had died during child birth owing to physical weakness and tender age and so had the baby. Ramesh wasn't really well-to-do, but to clinch this deal as Malati was both young and beautiful, he agreed to waive off all their loans as a wedding gift.

The fear of poverty is the biggest deformity of the human soul.

It maims all the innocence, purity and beauty of the human heart. It softens the character such that greed is able to push its roots into it. The roots spread out like fangs clasping, stifling, and choking everything that is simple and good in a human being. This greed is blind. It recognises no feelings, no emotions, and no relationships. It deadens all sensitivity, and its invisible worms turn the victim into a leper, who loses all his sensations of hurt and pain.

And it is at a moment like this, that a woman awakens to the fact that hers is a life of a slave. All the façade crumbles down in that one instant, all the charade is reduced to ashes. That which was brimming with life within her, that which was pulsatingly alive, dies forever. What remains after that is a breathing corpse which neither sees, nor hears and nor feels.

Thus it happened with Malati's mother, who just helplessly watched her child being sold off so cruelly, unfeelingly. For all the virtuousness and chastity that they had stressed all along, they themselves ended up selling their daughter to the highest bidder. Everything in her died at that moment of realisation of her servility and subservience.

For Malati too, it was the end of her dreams. She who was like a flower in the wilderness, blissful in her existence, she who was like a running brook full of joy and mirth, she who was like a whiff of fragrance enchantingly free and flowing; was now a bonded slave to someone who was offering her neither love nor a partnership of dreams but a life of drudgery and pain.

A deathly silence had enveloped her. Her heart became like the vast barren sandy desert, stretching from one end of her being to the other with no respite.

Despite all this, Malati and Ramesh were married off. At first Ramesh tried to reinvest in his fields, but the rains were still nowhere to be seen. Crops were failing again and again. Famine continued. So one fine day Ramesh announced that it was time for them now, to migrate to Lucknow. His cousin was already there in a slum settlement. He declared if nothing he could, at least pull a Rickshaw and earn two frugal meals a day.

This was how Malati came all the way to Lucknow teeming with people and noise from the vast open spaces of her peaceful Dausa.

There is something very phenomenal about the Hindu marriage. For all the reservation that one may harbour, for all the misgiving that one may hold, for all strangeness that may exist between the two unknown souls; something genuinely divine happens when the bride is handed over to the groom by her parents during the *Kanyadaan* and something equally mystic happens when they perambulate round the holy fire while taking the *Saptpadi* of marriage.

Malati must have experienced something similar because once married she surrendered all her thoughts, feelings and loyalty to the stranger who was now her husband. She worked hard from morning to night trying to make a home with whatever he earned. Incidentally Ramesh had by now got into a group of men who were heavily into drinking. It all started with an evening with friends as a special occasion. Then it became every weekend, then every other day. On coming back he would pick up a fight with her on some pretext or the other, to cover up his guilt, which would invariably end up with violence on her.

In the meantime they had a daughter Chiya, and Malati found that despite the autumn in her heart, a seed of hope was lying dormant inside her all the while and so were the songs of the spring.

She now wanted to live for her little one; she now wanted to live through her once again.

So she carried on, with a renewed desire, a renewed energy, a renewed hope.

And it was when Chiya was eight years old that Rama noticed Malati in that slum settlement. She came back and tempted her with the job offer. Malati needed the money desperately as by now Ramesh was drinking away nearly all his income, which wasn't much anyway, because the alcohol had taken its toll on his liver too.

Rama's irresistible charm, her extended hand of friendship and the financial offer were all so timely and that Malati grabbed them instantly and the turn of events finally landed her in my life like manna from heaven. It began as an amiable but an impersonal interaction more so because of my earlier experiences with maids which had left me wary of my own vulnerabilities.

However, the more I saw of her the more I realised that there was something in her that set her apart from all of the others, I've ever known. She had a refinement which could not be got by money, education or exposure and which no faded and darned sari could ever hide. Her approach to her work, her willingness to do all that she could like a member of the family instead of segregating her chores like jobs she was paid for and she wasn't, her integrity and absolute lack of greed; squeezed a grudging respect out of me and softly yet firmly established her in my heart.

I could actually match my clock to the peel of her doorbell early in the morning. Initially she'd just go about her chores softly, silently, efficiently and there would be hardly a question asked, a word spoken or information exchanged. But for someone like me who simply needs to connect with those in and around her life, the silence was proving to be both oppressive and asphyxiating. So one day while making my own tea, I made an extra one and offered it to her along with some Rusk biscuits. She demurred at first, but as I'd guessed, she was ravenous. I could see she hadn't eaten anything since maybe last night. Watching her have her tea with the suppressed intensity of a soul deprived yet too proud to admit her hunger, tore at my heart.

From then on every day, after all our chores were done, I would tell her to make tea for both of us. In the morning, while cooking for Vinay's lunch, a few extra chapatti would be stowed away to be later given to her with her favourite pickles and tea. Watching her eat hungrily was a bliss that made me often wonder if I hadn't already been her mother in some previous birth!

She seemed so slender and frail that I wondered if she ever had two proper meals a day. But then there was a space around her, I dared not violate. Moreover, I wanted her to open out to me, of her accord and trust.

Like a stray kitten who timidly eyes that bowl of milk at someone's doorstep for a long time before taking her first tentative and then eager steps towards it; I could sense her initial wariness slowly growing into trust and confidence. My concern and worry for her wiped away all the qualms that were possibly lurking in the dark corners of her silences and she appeared far more comfortable than before.

Often I would give her some of Nandini's dresses that she had outgrown and my saris which I felt would suit her better. It was at times like these that I would see brightness or a hint of a smile in her eyes as if to express how much this meant to her. Slowly she started getting Chiya along with her in the evenings as she was not very comfortable leaving her alone in the house now that she was growing up. Chiya who was around ten at that time, just a year younger to Nandini, came as a blessing for her, who would otherwise always complain how lonely and sad she felt at home, more so since she missed her old friends in Delhi. The two girls despite their disparities bonded so beautifully that it made me wonder where and how do we actually start learning to differentiate? They devised their own conversations and games and I would often find them playing

'School' with Nandini being the teacher at the blackboard or playing 'Shop' where Chiya would be the *Sabziwaali* and Nandini would be haggling like me.

Meanwhile, we two adults forged a deeper and more meaningful relationship altogether.

It was then that bit by bit I learnt about Malati's life starting from Dausa's vast, open and clean spaces until her coming down to the congestion, pollution, dirt and squalor of Lucknow.

I, in my turn shared my own childhood, the joys and excitement of growing up, our simple games, my love for books, the joy of becoming a lecturer in a Government college and then the agony of being forced to leave it all for my marriage. It was so easy talking to her. Her calm and quiet audience made words tumble out from the depths unknown, unexplored, unvisited ever before. She was my counter self, someone I could voice out anything to, without the fear of my being weighed, judged or laughed at.

Our conversations would often lead us to the shared burdens of womanhood, its huge demands on our singularity, the unfairness heaped on us from time to time, the pathos of being the second citizen no matter what, and the need for economic freedom as the very first step for empowerment in future.

These talks invariably stemmed out of agonies lived and felt deep within. There were days when I would catch her vainly covering her forehead with her pallu, in desperate attempt to hide the bruises of the previous night. Then the helpless look she'd give me when I'd ask piercingly, how much money had he decamped with last night, would tear my heart apart. I'd quietly slip in a hundred rupee note, when she'd be about to leave, knowing fully well that this would go towards buying their meager lunch and dinner for the day and maybe even stretched till tomorrow.

But what amazed me was her indefatigable spirits, her quintessential love for life, her inborn romanticism, the ideals that she clung on to despite having been cheated by life, time and again, despite being deprived, abused, battered and crushed at every step. Her boat of dreams, kept sinking right in front of her eyes, all her life; but she kept on clutching to its sides, her fingers bruised, lacerated, bleeding yet relentlessly unyielding in her hold.

Marriage for her was a sham, drudgery, an abuse yet she refused to give up her faith in its sanctity. She still believed it to be a bond of many births, a commitment to be honoured till the last breath and beyond. There'd be so many days when she would remain without a drop of water owing to some or the other fast that she had observed for the good health and long life of her husband; while performing all her duties with the same alacrity as ever. At times like these I'd be livid with her and would scream at her stupidity for killing herself slowly for someone who brutalised her day in and day out, who never showed an iota of tenderness or concern either for her or their little one.

She understood my pain but not my logic. With all the innocence in her eyes she'd explain that these were two absolutely different issues. He as a husband was free to choose the way he wanted to treat his wife, but that did not take away the divinity and grace of their bond. She firmly believed that we are puppets in the chains of destiny and all that we do or bear is governed by the commands of those chains. Strange it was to hear from her mouth a thought so profound that it had been voiced by none other than Omar Khayyam himself: 'The Moving Finger writes; and having, writ, Moves on: nor all your piety nor wit; Shall lure it back to cancel half a line; Nor all your tears wash out a word of it.'

I could buy her reasoning but not her resilience and forbearance. Such magnanimity was far too idealistic for me. However, I couldn't help but respect her for such fortitude and faith.

Being together in a house for many hours had made us privy to each other's sorrows and pains too. There were times when she witnessed my unexpressed anguish, times when Vinay would brush me off or snub me in front of outsiders for something so minor that it would hurt no end. Or like during one of my father's visits, he made his annoyance over a slight disagreement so obvious, his silence so vocal that it crushed me altogether. Much as I would try to hold back my tears, they would fall willfully at times like these, in the privacy of my kitchen, in front of the stove where there would be no one around. But she being a woman could sense my humiliation and shame without so much as a glance at me and I too would sense her mute sympathy and pain. She would later try to humour me by saying, "Didi you are so fortunate. At least Sahib does not drink nor stays out with friends till late night. Your Sahib is a saint didi, and you know, saints get angry easily just as they calm down easily too." I would end up smiling at this.

She was extremely fascinated by my having been a lecturer before marriage. She said it had always been her dream to teach young children, but owing to her early marriage she couldn't study beyond class eleventh. In Rajasthan Board in those days, the Senior Higher Secondary School was only till eleventh grade. So in a way she had completed her schooling. I often wondered why she hadn't applied for a better job in any organisation, school or college. I was certain she could easily be hired as a class fourth employee with better salary and perks. But she was certain that her husband would not approve of a proper job with long hours as he wanted her to be there in the house to serve him lunch and look after the child. But she was very keen to live her dreams through Chiya. She asked me solemnly one day if I could help her realise this dream. Her appeal was so sincere and intense, that I vowed to myself if God be on my side, I'd leave no stone unturned to make this one dream of hers, a reality.

From then on I started teaching Chiya personally along with Nandini. Chiya like her mother was a quick learner and had a passion for reading. So I'd let her take Nandini's old story books and magazines to pore over, in her free time. As I'd expected in just about a year Chiya had made up for the backlog in her education and was soon excelling in her class. Malati continued slogging in and outside her home, earning money for Ramesh to snatch away as and when he could – to drink it away and beat her when drunk.

Time thus went along peacefully for the next five years. We were by now firmly settled in Lucknow. I'd started writing weekly columns in the local newspapers and had also joined the Inner Wheel Club of Lucknow run by The Rotary, which gave me an opportunity to meet a large chunk of intelligentsia and professionals. Very soon it was time for Nandini's sixteenth birthday. We had planned a big event with her friends and ours. Both Nandini and Chiya were very excited about it. Nandini was insistent on having Chiya stay over for the night on her birthday. Malati, who was initially petrified of Ramesh's wrath on this subject, was finally forced to give in to the girls desperate pleas.

The evening went off beautifully. The food by the caterers was exceptionally good. Slowly the guests trickled away, the girls went to their room to open up the presents among giggles and laughter. I sat down with my cup of coffee to ease the swollen ankles. It was then that I noticed Malati running frenziedly all the way up my drive, bruised, bleeding and weeping uncontrollably. Before I could recollect my wits she was already at my feet like a wounded dove. I was simply paralysed to see her in this devastated state. Never had I seen her so broken and crushed. I begged her tell me the entire matter from the very beginning and whatever I could gather from her incoherent conversation laden with sobs and tears, left me stunned beyond words.

As was known Ramesh would often get his vile set of friends home for drinks. It was during one of these sessions that one of his drunkard friends who was already married with three children became besotted with Chiya. He blatantly announced in front of their group that he would have her at any price which Ramesh would care to name. And instead of being outraged Ramesh seemed delighted at this prospect. He just didn't find anything offensive about it as according to him that was how all marriages were fixed anyways. That was how he had got married and it had lasted him well. How it had lasted his wife was least of his concerns. Women were meant to be taken by men. This was their lot. All this fuss and drama, he said, was just because of the crazy books that Chiya was reading and which she too had once stupidly read. He shouted that it was precisely why he never liked the idea of their coming to my house.

This argument had been simmering between them for days, but that very evening Ramesh declared that he had fixed the marriage the coming Monday, *Akha Teej*, the most auspicious day of the Hindu Calendar. In Rajasthan it's a day for conducting marriages even if it was a child marriage or a marriage conducted without matching the horoscopes and that Malati had better get Chiya ready for it. Her refusal let to a fresh bout of violence leaving Malati battered, wounded and emotionally ravaged.

She begged me to save her Chiya from this plight and to grant them shelter for a few days. There was no way she'd let her husband's shadow fall on her little Chiya as long as she lived. This was a new Malati I'd never seen before. The woman who went without a drop of water for days to seek 'good health and long life' for her man, the woman who never answered him back, never ate before him, who would let him steal all her hard earned money for his drinks without a whimper, who took it as her lot to be beaten and abused; was now a tigress all out to protect her cub. And now it was written all over her that she would brook no threat, no violence, no force, and no coercion from anyone.

For the first time ever I peeped inside me to see who I really was. She had put me on an acid test. I was in a quandary, terrified of Vinay's reaction on one hand and challenged to honor my values on the other. It was time for me to take a stand. I finally walked up to Vinay and announced that I had decided to give them both a shelter and if he had any problem, I would be ready to move out of the house that very minute.

It must have been the determination written all over my face that did the trick, but I found that Vinay offered me no resistance. And once having made up his mind he went out calling the police officials he knew to seek their advice and help. Since Ramesh was a known drunkard and his friends small-time criminals, it was easy for the police to round them up and threaten them with dire consequences. Ramesh being a coward slunk away to his village for some days.

I took it upon myself to campaign for Malati's plight among all the academicians, opinion leaders and professionals I knew. It was then I realised that there is no power like that of women when they unite. In no time she got an offer for the job of an *ayah* in a well known residential public school. They even agreed to take in Chiya after seeing her glowing academic record.

Malati had to say goodbye to me, although deep down she knew there could be no goodbyes for the two of us.

While going away she was crying unabashedly but somehow I knew that all her sorrows were now over and done with. In her eyes I could see fresh magical hues of hopes and dreams and shimmering over them all, were a thousand rainbows of joy.

✦ ✦ ✦

2

Lessons of Life

Some are born with buck teeth, some with flat foot and some with an unquenchable thirst of love in their soul. Vishnu was born with the last of the lot and he had learnt to live with his cravings just as most of us learn to live with our deformities.

Vishnu had no idea of his age. No one talked about him in Malaunj, the lush green valley of Kumaon with Ranikhet on one side and Dwarahat on the other and with *Vaishnavi Mata Bhagwati Jagdamba* looking down on the *Ghaati* from Dunagiri temple at the top of the hill serenely.

No one ever reminisced about his birth, for his was an inauspicious birth under the *Mool Nakshatra*; the nineteenth constellation out of the twenty seven constellations of the Hindu Vedic Zodiac Science. A child born under this Nakshatra causes immediate demise of his father, mother or close relatives. True to the Vedic Shastras, Vishnu's *Ija* died trying to bring her little one to life which was anyway quite common then in Kumaon and his *Babu* contracted Tuberculosis and died two years after.

Within two years of his birth, a child who should have been the joy and life of the entire family had become a curse and a burden to those connected to him. Except for his grandmother *Aama* who was the mother reincarnate for that orphaned soul.

His father's was a joint family, as were all the rest in that valley, consisting of Aama, her three sons and their families. The three daughters of the family had all been married off to distant villages. With an agricultural land of 360 *nalis,* which was about 18 acres, they came under fairly well to do families of that area.

Aama's tenderness for Vishnu turned out to be a bone of contention between the other two brothers and their wives. They would've been extremely happy if he too could have joined his parents in their journey to the divine land, but unfortunately that was not to be and he was left behind as an additional, undesirable co-heir of the property. As was expected he was always ignored and made to feel unwanted.

As a toddler he would often take refuge in Aama's room or trail behind her wherever she went which would often be to the *Devta's Thyaan* or the *Chauka.* He'd watch her bathing the idols of Gods in a small brass plate, a piece of the holy five utensils for worship the *Panch Paatra,* chanting *shlokas* and then doing the *Aarti* with lighted lamp in one hand and the tinkling bell in another.

In the nights, he would cuddle into her, melting away in her soft hugeness with the bliss of the parched earth which has just felt the first showers of rain. And she would stroke him with the compassion of a quintessential mother calling out to him in her dialect *"Myaar baachh... myaar baachh!"*. She'd tell him stories of Lord Rama who was exiled into the forest by his conniving step-mother, the ten headed king of devils *Ravana* whom Rama killed, the monkey faced brave and loyal God Hanuman, the mischievous God with the flute 'Krishna', of Krishna's innumerable antics and the mock anger of his foster mother Yashoda. While swaying in half slumber, to the soft rhythm of those tales, he would often see himself chasing the golden deer in the woods, flying over the sea to reach the golden Lanka of Ravana, meeting *Sita Maiyya* and later blazing the entire Lanka to ashes with his burning tail. Sometimes he would see himself as the young mischievous Krishna eating the fresh soft butter from the earthen pots and dancing on the head of *Kaliya,* the mythological serpent with hundred and ten hoods who poisoned the waters of Yamuna and terrorised the entire Vrindavan village, till it cried for mercy.

However his most cherished memories were moments spent in that large, airy kitchen where the streaming rays of the sun would make Aama appear more beautiful and fairer than ever before. The golden beam on her silver hair would make them shimmer in a thousand hues while she would be engrossed in frying *Singhal,* spiral shaped semolina confection by pouring out its thick batter into a wok of hot ghee, with the curve of her palm – artfully and effortlessly; its ambrosial, appetising aroma wafting over him, teasing his senses and embracing him in a deep sense of belonging. Or when she would be chopping and cutting vegetables on the *daraanti,* a sickle with a wooden handle. Squatting on the floor she'd press the handle of the daraanti with her foot and using both her hands to hold the vegetables she'd chop them with a dexterity that comes with years of experience and practice. In the entire village there wasn't a soul who could challenge the taste of her *aaloo ke gutuka, ras, dubuk, churkaanii* or that crispy hot *Mandua ki roti* cooked on the slow fire of the *angithi* with dollops of homemade ghee served right on top of it.

For Vishnu who would sit near Aama for hours on end, these were his first lessons in life.

Life like a potter is forever kneading, rolling, mixing, pinching, throwing, trimming, carving, incising, pressing and moulding us into human beings of varied individualities, psyche, complexes, disposition and temperaments. It is the convoluted circumstances, the relentless realities, the cruel twists of fate that often shape us into the anomalous pots that we finally become. A childhood starved of basic parenting, a sense of being wanted, of the security of having someone to fall back on, can be very mutilating.

As he grew up Vishnu would try to please everyone around him. He would jump on the first call by any of his uncles or aunts, willing to run any errand they desired, always courteous and obedient to the point that stretched up to servility and meekness. But as was his wont, he was a convenience used without any emotion, used and discarded like the core of a consumed apple.

When the aunts needed *Bel Patras* for their Shiva puja, it was Vishnu who'd be asked to go to the village and hunt for 108 perfect unbroken sets from the trees all over. And he would willingly and enthusiastically collect them by walking for hours together trying to locate the trees, jumping, climbing, falling, grazing and getting pierced by the thorns on the branches, blood oozing out. Yet when he would present the purest 108 sets to them, with joy and hope in his eyes, he would be asked indifferently to leave them in the courtyard without as much as a kind look or a warm smile. Each such hurt made a dent he was unaware of, each hurt raked his heart and planted a demon there, each hurt left him still more ravenous and still more parched for love. Such were the lessons life taught him next.

Yet Vishnu had an intrinsic sweetness about him, a purity of heart that is possible only to those who are artless, guileless and honest. Above all, he had an essential faith in the goodness of life which was what spared him from bitterness and anger. He would forget a harsh word, an abuse, an ill treatment in no time and there'd be no shadow or tinge of animosity within him for anyone.

He loved life with all its shortcomings embracing his deprivations with perfect equanimity and contentment. He felt blessed in that 'little' which he could extract out of his life and felt alive to each and every bounty of nature and destiny. He loved running through the lush green meadows breathing in the cool pine air, watching the beauty of his lovely valley, the green slopes turn to dark rocks as they vaulted into the deep blue skies and the trees laden with the bright red *Buransh* flowers sway to the blowing breeze. He loved plucking *Kafal, Kirmoli, Hisalu, Bedu* right out of their shrubs, bushes, trees and biting into their juicy ripeness.

Thus life floated by. Days merging into months and months into years, till came the winters, the likes of which one had never seen before. It was a severely bitter winter, almost brutal; the winds so icy cold that they could cut right through your bones with the ease of a knife going into soft butter. In some weeks it started snowing relentlessly. The soft snow flakes fell incessantly all through the night, covering the entire landscape into its white nothingness. Vishnu could hear Aama coughing through the night, gasping for breath. She would mix some powder that the local Vaidya had given her with honey and take it regularly, but there appeared no relief in her ailment. Some nights she would be burning with high fever and on some days she'd appear her old cheerful self again. Vishnu found both his uncles *Jeth Baajyu* and *Kakka* (the elder and the younger brother of his father respectively) coming in to Aama's room more frequently now. At times he would hear some arguments and Aama's distressed voice followed by Jeth baajyu's soothing tone.

Vishnu hovered around Aama keeping a strict vigil on her needs and requirements. At times he found her staring at him with a lost helpless look, at times with unshed tears in her large rheumy eyes, at times she would call out to him and pull him to her bosom stroking him and moaning "*Myaar baachh*!... Myaar baachh!"

He could feel a lump in his throat, which was too painful for him to understand or bear.

One day she woke him up much before sunrise and informed him that as it was *Makar Sakranti*, they would both be going to Dunagiri temple in the jeep that his Kakka had arranged for them. She gave him a new set of clothes to wear and very soon they were on their way to the holy pilgrim. The fresh morning breeze along with the joy of watching the new sun bless the earth in all its splendour and glory was an exhilarating experience. Walking up the 365 steps was an arduous task especially for Aama who'd sit down every now and then. Once up there in the temple she seemed so ecstatic and blissful that all the toil and pain was forgotten. She informed the priest that her grandson had completed eleven years and that would he please perform his *Upnayan* right then.

So with a *havan* performed in front of the divine *Vaishnavi Ma*, with the holy chantings by the priest of that mystic abode, with the fruits, sweets, gifts and money that Aama had brought with her, with the limitless expanse of the sky, the earth and the Nanda Devi peak of the Himalayas as witness, Vishnu was initiated as the Brahmin or *Dwij*. He could now perform all the religious rituals and ceremonies as desired of a Brahmin man.

Thus with his ears pierced, head shaved barring a small thin braid at the back of his head and the sacred thread, *Janeu* round his neck, Vishnu came back with Aama, a much matured and grown up boy than before. The whole outing and climbing seemed to have taken its toll on the old lady's health and she lay down that night with a very high temperature and incessant cough. The entire family was outraged on finding the real reason and the ensuing repercussions of this journey. Vishnu was made to feel a culprit and he was too scared of them to offer any defense.

Aama's bouts of fever suddenly became more frequent and subsequently persistent going from mild to very high temperature accompanied by shaking chills, shortness of breath and sharp and stabbing chest pain. Her cough which was initially dry worsened into cough with thick yellow mucous and bloody sputum. Her health deteriorated every day and around a fortnight after, she could open her eyes no more. Her soul had flown away on its final journey in the middle of the night quietly and peacefully.

Everything after that was wrapped in a hazy vision for Vishnu. There was a lot of wailing and crying all around, the final ceremonies and a whole lot of new faces whom he had never seen before but who, according to his cousins, were members of their family and had come to be with them till their period of mourning or *Sootak*.

Vishnu would often retreat into Aama's room when the crowd would get too much for him to handle. He felt so bereft and lonely, so choked and suffocated. The feeling was yet to sink in and he wanted the denial to continue. He had not shed a tear nor spoken a word since she had gone and he hoped that he too could join Aama wherever she was.

It was at one such moment that he heard 'her' for the first time. "So you are Vishnu, aren't you?" It was a lovely, sweet, tinkling voice and he looked up speechless. She was elderly although not much and she had such a striking resemblance to Aama that it was unbelievable. He looked on incredulously. Finally, it was she who moved and stroked his head with far more understanding and tenderness than he had ever known from anyone else. She said in a voice so soft, "Aama used to write to me about you. She was very worried that you would not be able to bear her going away. You loved her very much, didn't you?"

Vishnu was not sure how it happened, but her words seemed to have detonated all that was choked in him. He simply broke down like a small baby, all his pent up emotions rushing out with a force that shocked him completely. Everything he was trying to deny all long, all that he was trying to hold back till now; surged out without any restraint or shame.

She hugged him so lovingly and naturally, his head on her bosom and let him weep unabashedly, uncontrollably without a word of remonstration or advice.

Much later when the tears had turned into dry sobs and then to a melancholic silence; did she strike him on his head lovingly and leave him to get him some water and food. Slowly she fed him, all the while talking in her soothing voice, which was like a balm on his frayed nerves.

She smiled as she spoke, "Oh! I am Aama's niece you know. She and my mother were twin sisters. Both of them looked identical. Incidentally I too am a spitting image of my mother. So no wonder you were shocked."

Slowly she drew him out from his shell and he found himself answering her first in the monosyllables then in broken sentences and finally after a couple of days he was talking to her, like he had never talked to anybody ever before.

She in turn told him about herself. She was Uma Tiwari and her husband Umesh Tiwari was a retired Engineer from the State Electricity Department. Their two sons were in Seattle and New Jersey and their daughter was married and living in Gurgaon. She said, "Vishnu, I too feel very lonely and lost without my children. My whole life had revolved around them for so many years. But what is the alternative beta? *Jehi vidhi raakhe Rama tehi vidhi rahiye.*"

There was such a charm in her voice and such wisdom in her speech that he couldn't but be drawn to her like a moth to a flame. Her presence filled him up with such tranquility of the soul that it was indescribable. The child in him clung to the mother in her and she too was drawn to his vulnerability and desperation.

It was during the mourning period that his eldest uncle, *Jeth baajyu* announced to everyone, "Ija had signed the property papers dividing the entire estate between me and *Kakku*. Since

Vishnu is still a minor we told her that we will have to look after him and his needs. After all that too is a huge responsibility. As one of the children living in our house, why should he be a separate beneficiary?"

Vishnu was still too young and innocent to grasp the complete weight of this fraud and duplicity. All he could recall was Aama staring at him with that lost helpless look, days before her demise, Aama with unshed tears in her large rheumy eyes, Aama pulling him to her bosom stroking him and moaning "Myaar baachh!... Myaar baachh!"

And he just broke down again and again, weeping inconsolably for the one who would never come back.

Uma could gauge the undercurrents in the family. It did not need a genius to realise that they had fleeced him of his rightful share and as things stood he was unwanted and unwelcome in that house.

Every day morning she would be woken up to the voices of, "Vishnu, have you chopped the wood?" or "Vishnu, go check the water boiler in the courtyard. And while you are at it get me a fresh towel too." If he was not running errands for someone, he would be in the kitchen cleaning *Laaii* for *Jethja* to cook for lunch or grinding chutney on the *Sil Batta* or sitting in front of the wok stirring the *ras* as it cooked on slow fire.

One afternoon she caught him in the kitchen.

"Vishnu are you going to do this all life long? Why don't you study?" she queried.

"No one ever sent me to school you see. They say I won't be able to study."

"Oh! that's not true at all. You have a very sharp mind. You know so many Sanskrit shlokas, don't you?"

"But that's different. Those I know as Aama chanted them every day."

"Well, that's how you learn other things too Vishnu. Okay tell me, would you like to study?"

He was speechless for a minute. Oh! To be able to study like his cousins. To feel worthy and knowledgeable just like them.

It just sounded too good to be true.

She was smiling at him, "Vishnu! Come over to Delhi with us. Live with us as our son. The house is so empty with my own having flown away to foreign lands. We'll look after you; teach you and one day you'll be able to stand on your own feet. Think about it."

He couldn't sleep the entire night. The very thought of going away was so incredibly fascinating that it frightened him just as it thrilled him too.

For the first time he sat down and weighed his life and the bonds that bound him. Without Aama there was no joy in his life anyway. There was nothing that pulled him back to his soil. This new choice was at least offering him warmth, education and a chance to stand on his feet. She was Aama's niece, so much like her. Being with her would be like having something of Aama to hold on to.

The more he thought, the more his conviction grew. Going away would give him a reason to live, a chance to heal himself. The next morning dawned on him with golden promise of a new life. Backed by his consent Uma informed his uncles that she and her husband would like to take Vishnu to Delhi. "We'd like to look after him and educate him. It's surprising that he has not been admitted to any school till date. He is such a bright boy and I don't see why he should not be given a chance to build his own future. Aama's soul, as it is watching us, would desire the same for him."

Her last statement was her final trump card and Uma knew it.

His, was a responsibility the family did not want to bear in any case. So letting him go was not an emotional decision for them at all. In the end it actually turned out to be a very smooth and an apathetic farewell for him.

Leaving Malaunj tore away at his heart, despite the hope of a new life. He watched tearfully the lush green fields for the last time, branches drooping with the weight of Buransh flowers swaying in the winds, waving good bye; the Kaphal trees looking on beseechingly as if to say: Stay till the *Chaita* my son. He watched his Malaunj as the car sped by, till it became a speck and finally disappeared from his vision altogether. Umesh ji and Uma understood his anguish and let him shed his tears in the privacy of the back seat.

Duplicity, rejection, parting, the pain of being uprooted, life's transience all came alive for him in the span of a day. This was yet another lesson of life.

Delhi came as a visual trauma for the young boy unexposed to the crowd, noise, pollution and chaos of a metro. He was terrified by the surging traffic and sat throughout in a shocked silence, too scared to utter a word. Finally he was introduced to his new home in Vasant Kunj. Uma went out of her way to ease his nervousness and fear. The house itself was very simply and tastefully done and had a welcoming aura to it. But what really surprised Vishnu was the matchbox like constructions of houses in such a huge city and the unbelievable paucity of space in these houses. He could not help but notice that the

Chauka in Malunj itself, was equal to half the apartment the Tiwaris lived in.

His meager belongings were accommodated in the spare bedroom which appeared so strange and small to him blocking his movements at every third step.

Nevertheless, he was overwhelmed at their willingness to embrace him in their fold, especially after the way his own family had deceived and rejected him so heartlessly. He knew there was no way he would not have stayed back if any of his uncle or aunt had said just once, *"Cheylaa nee jaa! Cheylaa nee jaa!"*.

He knew that back then, he was craving for that one gesture, one look, one pull of an arm which would have turned him back, no matter what the temptation; but they denied him his last straw.

Every day in the deep solitude of night, that burning shame of rejection, melted away the frozen pain in his chest, drenching his pillow drop by drop.

However as the days passed, the warmth and simplicity of this elderly couple who'd taken over the reins of his life wiped away all the hurt and agony of his exile.

It took him about a month to get adjusted to his new surroundings, his room and to think of their home as his own.

One morning Uma asked him lovingly, "Vishnu would you not like to call me Ija and Tiwari ji your *Bauji*? After all you are now our son, aren't you?"

These were phenomenal words for him. He was moved to tears. This was so unexpected and beautiful; he just could not believe it. To feel that someone thought of him as a child to be loved and cared for. After so many years, he also would have parents of his own. No longer would he be an orphan or the inauspicious one. He too would have a sense of security, the confidence of knowing that there are people he could fall back on, people he could call his very own.

The all consuming craving for affection and love leapt up in the heart once again. Once again in life, flared up the irrepressible urge to belong. Once again the yearnings sketched out a thousand dreams.

And so they became Ija and Bauji after a few diffident trials.

The impact of words are often underestimated. The mere change of address brought about an entire transformation in his heart. His whole being pulsated with a new sense of belonging, a sense of being wanted, loved and needed. It also brought in him a new sense of responsibility and commitment.

Meanwhile Bauji tried to look around for a school which would accept Vishnu as a student. The schools however expressed their inability to grant him admission as he had no educational background to speak of. The only solution left was to teach him at home and bring him up to a level equivalent to the other students of his age. And then subject to successful clearance of required examinations, admission could be sought.

So after giving it some thought, Bauji called him up and said, "Vishnu, I'll teach you myself from today onwards but you will have to be very sincere and committed. It is not going to be easy. However, it is not impossible either. I simply need your assurance that you will work hard." Vishnu eagerly promised him obedience, discipline and commitment.

From then on, he would get up early in the morning and learn his tables and grammar diligently. Bauji was very happy to see him working hard. He chalked out a schedule wherein he would teach Vishnu in the afternoons, when all was quiet in the house, the maids had completed their chores and left; and in the mornings, he would be required to learn his lessons and do his assignments. The arrangement worked wonderfully for about a month or so. The schedule was adhered to in all earnestness, but then as it often happens there came a glitch.

One fine day Ija announced that her maid had contracted typhoid and she would have to do all the household chores herself. Vishnu would have none of it. "No Ija! Not when I'm around."

She protested, but after a whole lot of argument, conceded to let him do whatever he could.

So from next day onwards, he took up the entire charge of the cleaning, washing, dusting, swabbing, while Ija concentrated on the cooking. She had never been very fond of cooking and had offloaded this responsibility on the maid long time back, so when she had to do it all over again, she found it extremely cumbersome. Vishnu could sense her discomfort over the next couple of days and without a word took over this obligation too, as one should in one's own home. He was an excellent cook having watched Aama so closely and keenly all his life till then.

He did not really mind giving up his studies as he felt that 'being family' meant feeling for each other, being together through thick and thin, it meant giving up one's selfish interests for the larger good of all, it meant making sacrifices with full conviction – willingly and joyously.

Ija was truly overcome and blessed him again and again, "*Jee reh, bachi reh – Cheylaa!* It is such a joy to have a son like you my child." And he realised that, he had never before felt so complete.

Initially Bauji would take Vishnu along, while making his trips to the local market. But over a few months, Vishnu had become confident enough to make his own independent trips and would volunteer as and when the need arose. He also became familiar with the local *Mandi*.

Slowly and steadily he started shouldering all their responsibilities out of intense love and regard for them. Although in this process his education got completely neglected, was a fact, no one noticed.

Both Ija and Bauji were thrilled to have him around and would love to show him off to all and everyone who dropped into their house. He had already been introduced to their neighbours and friends as just like our son. At such times he would secretly wish, he could wipe out the 'just like' altogether.

Their daughter and the youngest child Beenadi would often come over on the weekends from Gurgaon which was a forty minutes drive from their house. She was an equally warm and loving soul and would never forget to thank him for all his kindness and service to Ija and Bauji. The two sons would ring up once a fortnight religiously which pleased the two elderly no end. Vishnu was a stranger for both of them so they neither talked to him nor asked about him.

The elder one had married an NRI and had taken up American citizenship, while the younger one had already announced his intentions of marrying his colleague, an American Christian so as to apply for a Green Card thereafter.

All this sounded very alien and incomprehensible to Vishnu. Why would one want to leave one's own parents, one's motherland and all the love that was so abundantly available for strange, unknown places and people; he really could not understand.

What he sensed but could not decode then, were that these were the indicators of a shifting paradigm of the entire concept of family and bonds in these changing times. This shift was also responsible for the sowing of much insecurity deep within the soil of many an aging heart including Ija and Bauji's.

Once in a while Ija would talk about the heartache of having your own child turn into a stranger. The torment of looking at the face one had carried within one's womb for nine months or seen from the first wail onwards turning absolutely unfamiliar and unknown. His thoughts, his words, his beliefs appearing so deviant that one just could not connect with him anymore; leading to widening chasm of silence that swallows every communication between.

Vishnu would listen to her in all earnestness becoming of such somber and serious tête-à-tête and would nod his head gravely, although he really could not understand the meaning behind those words.

All this while he kept missing his lovely village. He wrote letters to his uncle and cousins and as expected did not receive a single reply. It hurt him terribly. Why ever did they not like him at all? Why this antagonism? What harm did he ever do to anyone? Why did he have to always grovel and beg for love, which everyone else got as their due?

Hot tears scalded his eyes as they coursed down the cheeks, meandering for an answer.

Their maid came a month after only to inform them that she was going back to her village for good. Ija paid out her dues and gave her an old sari as a parting gift. The matter was considered closed and over.

Life continued peacefully and comfortably with Vishnu looking after the chores and Ija doing whatever little she could on her part. The mornings and afternoons were occupied with domestic duties. In the evenings Vishnu would sit and watch the Television with Ija.

Bauji would go out daily for his evening walks and after that on alternate days for Bridge sessions.

Eight years flew by and Vishnu still felt as if he had left Malaunj just yesterday. He would still cry out for Aama in the dark loneliness of his nights. The wounds were raw and the pain still fresh. The healing he had hoped for never really happened. As he kept growing older he realised, that losing someone so essential is a wound that never heals. It just sinks deep, deep down. We foolishly assume that it has vanished. But it exists, throbbing with excruciating intensity, too adamant to die, too brazen to lie low.

Over these years Ija and Bauji had both weakened in health. Ija had developed diabetes which the doctor said was stress related although she did her meditations and *pranayams* religiously. Bauji said this was because she missed her two sons terribly and would not express it.

The elder one Deepak dadda had come just once in the last eight years and even then he did not have the leisure to spend time with his mother for a day. After all he had so many commitments to fulfill, taking his wife and children out for sight seeing, shopping, meeting up with old friends, exchanging notes about their mutual career graphs and dining out at all exclusive joints in the city. The greatest excitement of all being their trip to Taj Mahal. The poor mother was far too banal to be bothered about or to waste their precious time on. Her only utility being the dishes that she could be asked to cook for the benefit of sweet nostalgia and fond memories.

Over the years, bauji had developed conditions like high blood pressure and spondylitis but was very careless about his medications. One morning as he was leaving for his walk, he suddenly swayed and fell on the ground. Ija screamed and screamed till Vishnu came out to see what had happened. He immediately rang up the family doctor who came over in minutes, checked him up and declared that it was a very bad paralytic stroke. The next few days went in a whirl of activities, running back and forth from home to the hospital and managing both with equal agility while every fiber and sinew screamed for rest.

Bauji came back home after ten days of Intensive Care from the hospital as the shadow of a man he once was. Reduced to a life on bed he would look around so dejectedly and helplessly that his misery would cut right through Vishnu's heart. He tried to keep a cheerful front in bauji's presence but ended up shedding copious tears in the privacy of the kitchen.

Ija too was in a state of sheer distress which he knew could be extremely bad for her *sugar*. So the entire lot of handling one serious patient along with another potential one and the complete domestic responsibility from the payment of bills, going to the market to cleaning, washing and cooking fell squarely on his shoulders.

Since bauji was completely bed ridden Vishnu had to be a full time nurse too. Right from picking him up and taking him to the washroom every time he needed to relieve himself, he had to clean him up, bathe him, change him, feed him and give him his medicines as instructed by the doctor. He would spend hours massaging his inactive limbs in the hope that there may be some movement in them one day. All this demanded extraordinary strength and exemplary will power, both of which did not appear lacking in Vishnu.

Ija would often embrace him and say, "I may have two sons of my womb Vishnu, but trust me you are the only real son we both have – the son who's stood by us, the one who's doing his actual duty. You are the son who's been my strength, my courage, my support in these months of crisis. I want you to be my son in every birth of mine."

Her words were like the magic potion that refueled his determination and will power every time – all over again.

The two sons called every week now but both were too busy to make a trip to India. If for anything they would snap at their mother was to blame her for not agreeing to migrate to the States with them that created additional problems for them. After every such call, Ija's sniffles could be heard from her bedroom for quite some time. It was at moments like these that Vishnu would feel annoyed and disgusted with both her sons, for being so self centered and insensitive; but knowing what a mother's heart felt like, he'd swallow his repugnance silently.

Come winter bauji's situation worsened. The doctors tried their best to save him, but his vitals had started failing and finally on the tenth of December he breathed his last in his own home as he had always desired.

By next day both the sons had flown down to India without their families. Beena di had been there from the day Bauji's left for his heavenly abode. Ija was absolutely devastated and so was Vishnu, but he could not afford the luxury of tears as he was responsible for the entire running of the home, all the necessary rituals, their arrangements and also for Ija's condition.

He was so relieved to see his two foster brothers for he felt that now they would take care of everything.

But it did not take him long to realise that for his two brothers, he was definitely not family. As they came over and took charge, they made it very evident to him and everyone else in the house that for them Vishnu was just an outsider at best and a 'help' at worst. They would sit with Ija in her bedroom discussing important arrangements and matters with the door categorically closed on his face. Their conversations even in front of him would be in cryptic tones and what bewildered him most was that not only Ija was unfeeling of this discrimination but was as willing a party in the entire act.

It was also made evident to him, that he was expected to carry on with the cleaning, dusting, swabbing, cooking and serving just as though it was his duty. During the dinner while sitting down on the table, he was very distinctly advised to eat in the kitchen as they would be expecting other family members who were constantly in and out of the house, owing to it being the mourning period.

Vishnu was hurt by the way the two sons were treating him, but not shatteringly so. Ideally they should have felt grateful and obliged by the way Vishnu had cared for their parents specially their ailing father. But Vishnu could never think so limitingly. As per his goodness of heart, the two boys owed no allegiance to him and were free to behave the way they wanted.

But what was unbearable was that one who had adopted him, if only emotionally as a son, suddenly seemed to have had a complete amnesia about their relationship. Ija's stance was sheer torture for him. The one who had requested him to think of her as his own mother, call her by that name, the one who wanted him as a son in every birth of hers, had forgotten all about him, once his utility was over.

Accepting the rejection and duplicity of his uncles and aunts was still more tolerable as they had never wrapped their feelings in the silken folds of love and relationship. At least they had been honest and upfront about their apathy all along. But this, was simply cruel, simply inhuman. This was a disillusionment that crippled a person's psyche for life, crushed his trust and faith in every single bond, in every relationship. The more he mulled over this deception, the more his heart broke, the more emotionally battered he felt.

Suddenly the house seemed to be closing on him, he felt suffocated, choked, asphyxiated. His own inadequacy, his helplessness stabbed at his heart and he could feel tears stinging in his eyes like hot burning lava ready to burst out any moment.

Meanwhile he could hear the family talking animatedly in the next room, could hear Deepak dadda's voice, "Enough Ija, now we are not listening to you. It is not possible for us to drop everything at a moment's notice and come running all the way to India everytime you call us. Moreover I do not like the idea of your living with a stranger all alone in the house, no matter how nice he has been so far. In fact I must warn you that these boys from the hills are extremely crafty. They win you over with all their show of meekness, the drama of Ijaji, Bauji. And when they have finally earned your confidence, its then they strike. Every day I've been hearing or reading about how one or the other elderly has been robbed, mauled or murdered by their trusted servant. I'm sorry Ija, there's no way I can allow you to take this risk."

Vishnu stood stunned and frozen to the ground. Never in his wildest dreams had he ever thought that all his love, reverence, dedication of nine years would be razed down to this pathetic ugliness by the casual words of someone, who had not even earned the right to say it. And the one who knew better, who should have protested for his innocence had accepted those words silently. Blood sure was thicker than water and how!

He could not stay there a minute longer. He opened the door walked out on the street down below, tears streaming from his eyes, lungs gasping for breath. He had no idea how long he walked on blindly. He must have walked down to the association park and sat down on the bench as if on an auto pilot. It was a long time after, when their neighbour Mrs. Mathur spotted him sitting alone under a Gulmohar tree and walked up to him.

She was a very close friend of the Tiwaris and knew that Deepak was planning to take his mother to Seattle permanently this time. She and her husband had been watching Vishnu for the last nine years with their neighbours and had secretly marveled at his commitment and dedication. She had already decided to make him an offer at the earliest convenient moment and this one seemed to be just perfect, "Vishnu would you like to live with us, once your Ija has gone abroad? You know with our children married and away, the house seems so empty and sad."

Vishnu stared blankly in front of him, hearing the noises of the vehicle traffic, coming from the busy street ahead. The sky was the colour of the ash and a crow was cawing raucously from the parapet of a balcony close by. The world, Vishnu realised goes on. It just goes on whatever happens to one – anyone. He knew now he would have to live out his life all of his own making.

For a moment he felt like he was back in Malaunj, walking down the steps of Dunagiri temple, clutching Aama's hand. The red Buransh flowers were waving in the wind and the Kaphal trees were looking on beseechingly. Suddenly, Aama was gone and he could see himself cold and frightened going down those steps, down and down further, all alone in the land of mist and darkness.

✦ ✦ ✦

3

Lucknow Mail

Mrinalini

"Oh God! this terrible traffic and the pollution." I could feel the dust clinging to my face. The *pithiyaa* was already bleeding out, with the *akshat* on the pithyaa, moving away like canoes and if unchecked would have reached my nose very soon. Subconsciously, I wiped my face with the far end of my pallu inwardly flinching as I thought of what Naveen would have said at this rustic behaviour. The pallu had been smeared blood red and I could feel its crimson vaulting up and moving on to my cheeks out of sheer embarrassment for having been so hasty.

It had been a long day and standing here on the platform of the New Delhi Railway Station, waiting for the 10.30 p.m. 'Lucknow Mail', I could feel the sinews of my calf groaning with pain. Yet, I would not have exchanged this fatigue for all the leisure in the world.

Coming over to Maa's home in Delhi, after an inordinate gap of three years, had proved to be such an emotional experience that I could feel a lump in my throat even now. After *baba's* passing away, I somehow just could not bear to come back, although Naveen always said that Maa would need me far much more now, than ever. But the very idea of our home without baba was unbearable to me and coming here again would have just nailed the truth with a finality which I could not endure.

Unfortunately Maa had not been well for some time. Her blood pressure had shot up uncontrollably and she had to be hospitalised. *Bhaiyya* had somehow gauged that she was missing me but would not acknowledge it for the fear of disrupting our busy lives. So he and *bhabhi* called us up with a request to come over for a few days. Durga Puja being round the corner too, made the whole idea all the more attractive and feasible.

Naveen had a conference coming up in Chennai. However, he willingly conceded to take a short break before that, to be with us for the puja. He proposed that I could then stay over as long as I desired.

Thinking of Maa unwell filled me up with an inexplicable urge to be with her at the earliest, along with such an intense sense of remorse and shame. How could I have been so self absorbed as to forget that she was the one who had suffered the most. I somehow felt guilty and responsible for the state she was in and promised myself to make up for my apathy and to look after her and pamper her, as she truly deserved to be pampered at this juncture of her life.

Life had not been very easy for my mother. I still remember watching her as child, slogging in the house from morning till night, working relentlessly cleaning, washing, ironing, cooking for us without any help whatsoever. Those were our days of frugal living, for Baba had always been a person of integrity and high morals. As a professor, in those days, he commanded immense respect but meager salary. Those were incidentally the days when academicians like him considered teaching a mission. At times he would even invite some poor but worthy research scholars, more often than not of our own community, offering them free boarding, lodging, guidance and even taking care of them, as if they were his own kith and kin.

Although the brunt of this benevolence had to be borne by my poor mother who was required to forego a lot many necessities, stretching baba's paltry salary to meet the additional needs of our extended family. And while she did try to cloak her hardship from everyone including Baba under the veil of sweet serenity, there was just one person she stood absolutely exposed to, just one who was a witness to her embarrassments, her pains, her fears, her insecurities – me.

I would see her desperation after the 20th of every month, checking out the empty pockets of her purse again and again as if the next investigation might miraculously yield some hidden wealth, fumbling under the newspaper linings of her almirah shelves, or shaking out the folds of her saris to find any leftover cash that she had hidden in the beginning of the month but which the *Sursa* like ever widening needs of our home would consume in no time. I had seen her adding more water to the vegetables to increase their volume and make them go round sufficiently for all. I would marvel at her levels of sacrifice and tolerance and my concern for her would often get translated into my uncalled for ire against those poor research scholars.

These thoughts brought to mind the one set of brooding eyes I had made life hell for – the one student baba had loved above all and the one I had disliked the most – Aditya.

And also of how fate had laughed at me after that.

Aditya, just that name stirred up a sandstorm of memories, its dust flying into my eyes, stinging, burning, blurring everything, blinding me with my own tears; leaving behind a barren, desolate vastness deep within. But dodging it deftly I turned my thoughts back to Maa, and how very shocked I had been to see her once beaming, glowing face so pale, feeble and lusterless. Our arrival had coincided with her return from the hospital and with all the heavy medications having taken their toll on her, she appeared so lost and frail that it absolutely wrenched my heart.

Maa was ecstatic at our surprise visit and would touch my face again and again to make sure it was not a dream although I knew that the changed sombre me post marriage was someone both Baba and she had never been able to face. Much as I wanted to cloak it for their sake, I was never that good an actor to have carried it off with finesse.

When Naveen informed Maa that he would be there for the puja too and that I had to stay on further, for as long as she needed me, I could actually see tears shimmering in her eyes in a million hues.

Naveen had been Baba's choice for me out of all the prospective grooms that my uncles, aunts and Baba's friends had suggested. Baba had known his family for years and had watched him grow up into a man of strong values, kind, dependable and family oriented. Maa for whom baba's judgment was essentially unquestionable, had instinctively loved him on her own too.

As long as Naveen was there, maa would have him administer all her medicines. She was like a child with her favourite toy and would want to see him till her eyes drooped down in sleep. Strangely such sentimentality which Naveen otherwise brushed off in anyone else, from Maa, never irked him. In the one week that he stayed there, Maa's blood pressure had stabilised to its normal. Bhaiyya and bhabhi would often tease Maa and tell her, "What fools we were to let the hospitals fleece us with such exorbitant fees, when we could have had you hale and hearty with just one trip of your son-in-law."

Maa would show her mock anger at these banters, but I could see that she was elated to have Naveen around her.

After the festivities of Durga puja and Naveen's departure to Chennai, we got back to the rhythm of everyday life. I wanted to see Maa in perfect health, before I left and therefore made special efforts to keep her happy and relaxed. We would go out for short walks, sit in the balcony overlooking the lawns below. I would put on her favourite music and we would lose ourselves to the strains of Kumar Gandharv, Paluskar, Ajoy Chakravorty and talk of our earlier, happier memories. However, there were some memories I would not rake up for anything in the world. Memories that I had always shied from, memories that stabbed me deep within, memories which with every recollection twisted the blade mercilessly inside me.

Within a fortnight, Maa had regained the lost colours of her cheeks and had found some bounce in her steps back again. Then came the moment of parting for both of us, but this time I made her promise that she would come for Naveen's birthday on the 15th of December and stay with us for at least a month. She could then teach me how to make her special *chhaina paayas* for Naveen too. The trump I knew had been played and played well. How could she not agree?

After she had put the *pithyaa* on my forehead and I had touched her feet, she hugged me, held me for a second and whispered, "Chutki, try to be happy with what destiny has ordained for you. Stop clinging to your past. I've learnt it the hard way. There'r times when we should know how to let go."

I was speechless for a minute. So had she known it all along?

Or was it my guilt playing up? Who knows. I forced a smile and waved her good bye.

And now standing there waiting for the train in the oppressive heat caused by the hustle and bustle of the crowd, I kept wondering how time refuses to move when you most want it to.

Aditya:

Thank God I finally made it. I was not sure I would make it to the station in time, especially with that bumper to bumper traffic on the road.

How I dislike Delhi! Its pollution so thick that one can actually shake its hands, its traffic like an adamant mule refusing to go forward, roads with potholes and abnormally steep speed breakers, distances that appear like one is travelling from one town to another and the teeming population running frantically like a headless chicken.

Delhi which does not bother about people or rules or principles. Delhi where power and wealth are the only two currencies that run. Delhi which gives me a claustrophobia every time I am forced to bear with it. It is such a relief to be going back to Lucknow finally. In fact I was quite scared, I might not get a seat owing to my last minute get away, but strangely the Lucknow Mail seemed to have quite a lot of vacancy just tonight.

It had been a week since I had come to Delhi on a conference of 'Rethinking Indian Nationalism' organised by the University of Delhi. It was a great opportunity to meet and interact with some of the renowned scholars and professors of history from all over India. Normally I am quite reticent of sharing my works and writings on public forums. I would rather publish them in papers and books so that they are available to the academicians who genuinely want to read them. But our Dean had been very keen that I represent the Lucknow University and with all my regards for him I had no option but to fall in line.

We were put up as usual in the University Guest House at the Vishwa Vidyalaya Marg opposite the University gate. It was a week spent in enriching conversations, informally on various topics of Medieval History with fellow professors and formally on the theme of the conference.

The conference finished today evening and a celebratory dinner was announced for all the participants along with the Delhi University faculty. But really, I had had my fill of being away from Lucknow and it was using the excuse of sickness that I was able to make this get away at the last minute. What I had not realised was that these were the peak traffic hours for the Delhi roads, being the time when everyone returns back from work. So there were traffic jams all the way from North Campus, Delhi University to Ajmeri Gate Railway Station, resulting in my being able to catch the train just in the nick of the time as it started pulling away. At the ticket counter I had merely asked the man to put me in any comfortable coupe for all I needed was to sleep the night through.

As I stood at the gate of the AC First Class trying to get my breath back, I could see Delhi slipping behind me first inching away, moving behind the posh colonies, apartments, malls visible so distinctly, and finally rushing away as the public squalors, slums and the shanty towns flowed by, surging forward and away like a river in heavy monsoon.

Sometimes I wonder if it is really Delhi that irks me or the memories that it instinctively brings along?

Memories that are otherwise woven in every fiber, every nerve, every sinew of my body, memories that flow in every breath, resound in every heartbeat and yet I never acknowledge them.

Strangely, Delhi at one time was the only place I wanted to be in. It was a home I had never otherwise known with parents who were not mine, who had yet meant so much more.

Delhi at one time has innocence, mischief, laughter, and love.

Delhi at one time was a face that filled me up with a desire to live, a face with large dark eyes that would reflect a vignette of emotions so eloquently, eyes which boasted of a confidence that shrouded a million vulnerabilities, eyes that would tease me, laugh at me, show annoyance, anger, concern, tenderness and countless yearnings which the owner herself was too naïve to understand; eyes which I have carried in my heart all these years much to my own chagrin.

Yes! Delhi at one time was – Mrinalini.

Incidentally all I remember of my childhood are the vast fields of rice and corn in Barabanki District and the gently flowing Gomti. I was born to a middle class joint family although not a very big one. Much as I want to I cannot recall my mother who left us for the beyond when I was just a toddler. I was brought up by my aunts as a part of their own brood. My father, as fathers in those days were, did not indulge in or encourage demonstration of feelings and anyway there was enough for him to occupy his attention with, especially increasing losses of the farm, poor yields, need for another tractor, higher quality seeds, more fertilizers and so on. The emotional needs of a growing child was a luxury he really didn't had time for. When I was around five, I was enrolled in a school with the rest of my cousins. Luckily I took to studies as a duck would to water. With no guidance and no one to consult, I still managed to top my class every year.

Our principal must have sensed something bright in me and so he went all out to arrange for a scholarship for me from the board. He convinced my father to let me go to Lucknow for advanced studies. He went as far as to arrange for a hostel accommodation for me through one of his friends in Lucknow. My father found it very difficult to deny me the opportunity after all this and reluctantly agreed to let me indulge myself for a couple of more years, being quite sure that a farmer's son would get tired of books very soon and would want to come back to his fields.

However, I was wired differently. I had a passion for studies especially for History which enthralled me like nothing could. I went on to do my Masters in History from the prestigious

Lucknow University topping once again. By this time my father too understood that he would not be able to pull me back into his fields and so he declared that I was free to make my own life.

I wanted to do my research under my idol Prof. Nityanand Joshi, the doyen of Indian historians who was then teaching at Delhi University. When I went to him for the first time armed with my meager academic qualifications and my intense passion for the subject, he was extremely moved. Since the hostels were already full, I was forced to rent a *barsaati* near his house in South Delhi. To pay for my rent, food and books I started giving tuitions. Most of the tuitions available were of Higher Secondary students, where all that the parents wanted was a tutor who could make their self opinionated and spoilt teenagers, to sit down and study. This kind of work made me miserable, but my conscience would not permit me to seek financial help from my father. This additional burden of work compelled me to sit through the night to do my own studies. There was no way, I was going to disappoint my mentor and my guide.

Prof. Joshi was a man of mighty heart. He was a master of his subject but more than that he was a Guru after the old school of thought. It did not take him long to read the dark circle of my eyes, my emaciated look and the extra efforts I was putting in to complete my work. So one day he insisted on me packing my bags and coming over to his house to live with him and focus on my studies, without any worry of rent, food or books.

Both Prof. Joshi and his wife embraced me to their hearts like I was their own family. They were simple, warm people of high ideals and principles.

Having lived most of my life in hostels alone I had never known what it was to be cared for. I had never had anyone sitting up for me till I ate my food, no one concerned if I was stressed out or ill, no one with whom I could share my day's happenings with, no one to laugh or smile with. I had grown up into a reticent young man who found it very difficult to open out or relax. Suddenly I had a home to come back to, I had foster parents who cared about me like a child should be cared for, I had everything to make me feel blessed, except for one problem – their daughter Mrinalini (or Chutki as she was called at home).

Mrinalini, as I remembered her, was like a young river cascading from the mountains, surging forward to meet life with a vibrancy, a joy, a gay abandon possible only to liveliest and the purest of heart. However, she made it very obvious from the first day that I was an outsider, an unwelcome burden who was sponging on her parents' kindness and fleecing them of their hard earned money and hospitality. She would annoy me with her silly tantrums, like when Prof. Joshi would be discussing something very important, she'd barge into the room, seeking his attention just then or taking him away on some pretext. This would kill the entire tempo of the discussion and sometimes the discussion itself would get lost in the confusion. Or she'd tell her mother not to wait for me over lunch as she had heard me saying that I would be back late evening. On being asked I would not be able to refute her lest she got scolded, but it would hurt me terribly besides forcing me to undergo the agony of hunger.

However, once the acrimony was stretched a bit too far. Prof. Joshi found that there was some fault with the 'earthing' of a major switch board owing to which a fairly large amount of current was leaking. He instructed both Mrs. Joshi and Mrinalini not to let anyone operate that particular board till he sent someone to repair it as there could be a danger of electrocution. In the afternoon when I came back from the University library, I found that Mrs. Joshi had gone to the neighbours to see their ailing child and Mrinalini was reading a book in the living room without the fan. Thinking that she must have been too lazy to switch it on I remarked, "Why didn't you switch on the fan Chutki? It's really so stuffy. Wait I'll do it for you."

So saying I walked up to the switch board and strangely just for a moment turned back to look at her. She had a very shocked look on her face, mouth agape like she had something to say but did not. I pushed my hand towards the switch board, only to be pulled in and pushed back by an extremely powerful wave of current. It threw me down unconscious, my whole body shivering frenziedly, for how long I could not remember. All I remember was her scream, so very loud and then louder, her rushing up to me and after that a blank.

When I finally gained consciousness I was on the bed, Prof. Joshi at my bedside and Mrs. Joshi rubbing the soles of my feet. Fortunately it was just a mild shock, but Prof. Joshi said it could have been very serious too. I was asked to stay in bed for that day and drink lots of liquid. I could make out that Mrinalini had been severely reprimanded. I saw her peeping from behind the door several times.

That evening she came holding a tray of orange juice and fruits. "Maa wants you to eat them." Her voice was low and heavy and she appeared to have cried a lot too. She sat down to peel the apple and slice it, her eyes downcast, not daring to look up at all. Much as I was furious with her, after having known the truth, my heart went out to her for this unnecessary suffering and remorse. But I did not know how to make her comfortable, so I let it pass.

However, that evening I saw a new Mrinalini and I saw the sensitive, feeling, caring woman in her, someone she herself had never met before.

Over the days, she opened out to me, though I still was the same withdrawn soul, feeling terribly handicapped because of my inability to share myself with anyone. She proved to a bigger nuisance in friendship than before. The amount she talked made me want to tear out my hair. I would gently and firmly shove her out of my room to have some peace so that I could study but she'd be back in five minutes with another fresh piece of excitement.

In just a few months, I knew each of her friends by heart – how Manju can solve any Mathematical problem in minutes, how Sabaa has the sweetest voice I could have ever heard, how Neeru mimics their Hindi teacher just perfectly and so on, till I screamed for mercy.

But for all my show of annoyance; deep down I was surprised to see, how I loved it all!

For the first time someone had reached out to me with such softness, such innocence, such artlessness. For the first time someone opened out a world of joy and laughter for me. For the first time there was someone whose entire being lit up on seeing me.

With her brother away for the past one year in IIT Roorkee, she had felt an inexplicable loneliness. Now with me around she wanted to make up for all those lost moments with him as a companion.

In just a few days she made sure everyone knew that I was her personal property and if anyone wanted to reach me even if it was Mrs. Joshi, they would have to come through her.

So if Mrs. Joshi wanted to knit a sweater for me, she'd have to ask Mrinalini for the measurement of my arm or if hot *gujiyas* were being fried in the kitchen, then there was no way the first of the lot won't come straight to me hidden in her dupatta; and if in the process the dupatta became oily and she got scolded for it, she'd just screw up her nose and laugh.

And when she herself wanted to try out rolling the chapatis, the earliest lot of half cooked ones, the burnt ones were all stacked away for me to eat and dared I say no to them.

Prof. Joshi looked so relieved to have the matter between both of us 'sorted out sensibly' as he called it. He was also glad to see that now I could be trusted with odd jobs for her. So if it was her admission for M. A Economics it would be, 'Aditya please take her along and get it done.' Or 'Aditya, will you get her books from the University shop. Do also go to Prof. Sharma and ask him for the reference books she'd require.'

While she would use me as her armour against everyone, 'Aditya tell baba I won't do Economics, no way; even if he gets annoyed. You'll tell him Aditya, won't you?

I want to do my Masters in English only. You know even Sabaa is doing the same.

Please, Aditya!'

Wincing at being caught between the devil and the deep blue sea, I would grit my teeth and stand up against Prof. Joshi for her. How could I let her down?

Thus life carried on sweetly and wonderfully for the next few months.

And then the disaster struck, as it invariably does, out of the blue. Mrinalini was besieged with most excruciating headaches and frequent vomiting. For quite some time Mrs. Joshi tried the old and often tested home remedies. But when the headaches grew severe, the family doctor was called and she was diagnosed with Bacterial Meningitis of an advanced stage. The doctors termed it as an emergency. In fact they counseled Prof. Joshi that he must be mentally prepared for the worst, as this particular meningitis is often fatal and very few survive this ordeal.

Mrinalini was immediately shifted to the ICU and life changed so drastically for each one of us. Prof. Joshi shut himself behind a wall of icy silence refusing to allow anyone to peep into his boundless worries and abysmal anguish. Mrs. Joshi turned into a bundle of nerves with tears flowing out incessantly and lips busy in soundless prayers. Bhaiyya had his final examinations so it was decided to keep him in the dark till he had written all his papers. And I was like a zombie, running around from hospital to home and even the normal routine jobs which were earlier handled by Prof. Joshi came over to me due to his emotional withdrawal. Specialists were called in and the best possible treatment administered. But still there was no major improvement.

The doctors did not want to keep her in the ICU for very long for fear of septicemia and so she was shifted into a private room. But they informed us that she was still not completely out of danger. As Prof. Joshi suffered from hypertension, it was decided that I would stand guard in the hospital during the nights. It was during those vigils, those long hours of looking at her completely wan and lifeless face, during those seemingly endless moments of wondering what if they could not pull her through, that it flashed across my consciousness how desperately I needed her in my life, how essential she was to every breath that I drew, how I craved to see her smile, to hear her voice, to feel her breath close to me.

It was the fear of losing her that broke every caution, every restraint, every prudence in me which I had cultivated over all these years for my survival. In that moment of complete madness, of recklessness borne out of desperation, that I bent to, caress her hair with gentle hands, to feel her breath next to mine and before I knew, I found myself kissing her softly on her forehead, all my love kneeling at the pew of her altar. And suddenly as if someone had opened the gates of my dam, all my pent up emotions, the stress and the agony surged over with a force so powerful, so primal, so indomitable that tears gushed out from my eyes helplessly.

The drops as they fell down on her brought back a flicker at first, a tremor and then her eyelids opened slightly and she gazed into my tear filled eyes so close to her face that she could have touched me with her long eyelashes.

She gave me a weak smile and whispered, "You know, you don't look half as good when you cry."

I wanted to smile back and cover up for my indiscretion, but I just broke down and cried like I had never cried before. "Don't leave me Chutki," I sobbed, "I need you so badly. You're all I have, my love."

She lifted her frail hands and caressed my face with both her hands, trying vainly to wipe my tears and then finally with the depth and wisdom of a woman in love, she brought my face still closer and kissed me with all the love in her heart.

It was a kiss that lasted for just a moment but a moment that promised to stretch forever as long as I lived.

It was the moment of revelation, the moment of understanding, the moment of final surrender and we both clutched on to it like a drowning man clutches onto his last breath, like a dying man holds on tenaciously to the last thread of life, with all our longing for each other, the flaming intensity leaping up brazenly within.

There are times when words are so unnecessary, so incapable of holding the infiniteness of our feelings; times when the soul identifies and reaches out to its own self in someone else, when the eyes do the talking and the hearts whisper to each other.

In that one moment of midnight, within the walls of that hospital; we both knew that we had found our soul mates that we belonged to each other forever and ever.

We still do not know, if it was the medical care or our love for each other that gave Mrinalini a second lease of life, but it was definitely a miracle of miracles even in the words of her own doctor.

Once she came back home, I took it upon myself to see that she recouped as fast as possible. I personally administered her medicines, made sure she had her juices and milk as required and much to everyone's amazement, she did listen to me like a little lamb all through.

There was so much I wanted to say, but never did, my intrinsic shyness having found its way back to me once again. But I still managed to convey all that I felt, through a smile, a look or a touch that lingered on an instant more than needed. She'd often come into my room in the lazy afternoon of the long summer days and we'd just sit around talking, sharing with each other our most personal thoughts, longings, desires and dreams we had never voiced even to ourselves ever before. I would play her favourite Rafi songs for her on the tape recorder and we'd both lose ourselves to his mesmerising voice and the romantic lyrics; and just sometimes I'd reach out and caress her face, or she'd put her head on my shoulders shutting the entire world away from her eyes.

Our lives thus continued to sail peacefully, with my research work coming quite to its end and she becoming the fulcrum of my life, with all her joy, hope and smiles till Prof. Joshi returned from his conference in Lucknow. Over this period of time I had come very close to Prof. Joshi. I was his student, his secretary, his assistant. He did not write his papers anymore. Instead he would brief me on the paper that he had to read, he would give me the points he wanted to touch along with the references and I would prepare the draft of his paper. He'd then tone it up and give it a final shape.

This time when he came back from Lucknow, he patted my back and told me that the paper had been wonderfully written and was taken up for publication in a leading international journal. He also seemed very excited about having met his old friend and colleague Prof. Bhatt who invited him home for dinner. Prof. Joshi had been very fond of his family especially his son Naveen who had now become a Marketing Engineer in a leading Multinational firm.

Putting his arm around my shoulders in a very fatherly manner, Prof. Joshi confided, "Aditya, I've met Naveen and

I'm confident that he'll be a perfect match for our Chutki. I've known their family for years now, they're wonderful people and Naveen is a very good boy. But Aditya, you know our Chutki, she's such a headstrong girl although she's very soft and sensitive deep inside. But you know I can't handle histrionics and anyway you're the only one she listens to. So talk to her Aditya. Tell her its a very good match. He'll keep her happy. This is the only one thing I ask of you *beta*. Consider it my Guru Dakshina."

So saying he wiped off a stray tear from his eyes and I realised that Prof. Joshi had suddenly aged a lot in the last couple of days.

Being in a state of happiness is always like being in a trance. Its when the reality strikes us that the spell is broken and we come out of our reverie rudely awakened, disenchanted and bruised.

✦

Life plays its own truants on us. It lets us rise with our fantasies, lets us float in the magical space of ecstasy, lets us build those castles in the air and then pushes us down on the ground with a hard jolt.

The entire night a river inside me was flooded with nameless sorrows. The entire night my heart was wrenched at both ends. The entire night I cradled the shattered pieces of my dreams in my eyes – slivers slashing into their softness, tears oozing out, drenching my pillow ceaselessly. The entire night I was gasping for breath, choked, asphyxiated.

The next morning I called Mrinalini to my room. I took her hands in mine softly and pulled her near me. She looked up at me with immaculate innocence and surrender in her eyes. Mustering up all the tenderness I said, "I've never asked anything of you till now. Today if I want something, will you give to me Chutki?"

She smiled, all her adoration, all love bursting out from every fiber of her being, "Do you 'need' to ask Aditya? What is there in this life that is mine any longer?"

"Chutki I'm serious, you take your time and decide." I protested.

She said, "That would be trading Aditya, not offering. Isn't it? Whatever I had is already yours. So please tell me."

I told her about Naveen and her baba's fervent desire. As I was speaking I felt like a butcher taking the goat to its slaughter. Her face which was glowing with joy a few minutes back, had turned ashen and then slowly the white of death could be read all over it. I saw her face twitching with suppressed fury and then slowly a deadpan look which ripped my heart so brutally that I crumbled inside.

However I tried to carry on with nonchalance I did not feel, but she stopped me with her hand. In a voice which suddenly seemed orphaned she cried out mournfully, "How could you do this to me Aditya? Oh! The duplicity of it all – "Today if I want something, will you give to me Chutki?"

"You knew what you were asking for. Didn't you? You wanted my entire life, all my happiness, my very breath."

"Okay, now you have it, Go tell baba – Chutki will do anything I say. She'll walk on the coals for me."

Saying so she crumpled and fell on the ground wailing, lamenting, weeping unabashedly. I sat there like a log of wood.

After an hour or so she put her tear stained face on my knees and we both sat in that deathly silence till she dozed off tired and spent.

As expected Prof. Joshi was beyond himself with joy. For the entire next month, I was given a list of jobs everyday that kept me away from home nearly whole day long. When I entered home, Mrinalini would bring my dinner in the room, and when I would hold her arm to stop her from going away, she would sit down on the floor weeping silently.

From the day she had said, "OK, Now you have it, go tell baba – Chutki will do anything I say. She'll walk on the coals for me," I never heard another word from her. The effervescent, breezy, joyous girl who was like a cascade running down the snowy mountains chiming with laughter and glee had suddenly changed into a mute, lifeless doll.

Bhaiyya was called from his college, the relatives also started coming in. So meeting Mrinalini became impossible. A day before the wedding, I met Naveen and he was everything Prof. Joshi had said he would be. The entire family was very grounded and simple, which made me respect them all the more.

The ceremonies completed, Mrinalini left for her new home and all that I could have said was left unexpressed, unshared, buried inside the deep cervices of my heart.

Today as I left Delhi, those memories had surged up from nowhere bringing with them fresh debris of sorrow and anguish. The pace of the train had reached its peak. I could feel the cold air slapping my face. Time to turn in and sleep I thought and I proceeded to my coupe.

Mrinalini:

It had been an hour since the train had left the station. I had been informed that there was going to be one more passenger in this coupe. The very idea of being alone with a stranger for the whole night was both very disconcerting and scary. As the time passed I kept on hoping that maybe whoever it was had missed the train after all.

And just as I was zooming in on this possibility, he walked in.

Aditya? Oh yes it was Aditya alright.

Stunned, speechless; I froze like a deer caught in front of the headlights. I have no recall of what went through me at that point of time but I am quite sure I must have stared at him like I had seen a ghost. My eyes open fully wide, my face white as sheet, my hands cold and sweaty and I sans all consciousness of time, space and self.

Not a breath left my body for I do not know how long. Finally I heard him move and come near me, "Hey Mrinalini, what a surprise."

I managed a weak smile. And then yet another exclamation from him, this time a more distraught one, "Oh my God, but look at you. What have you done to yourself? You've not been keeping well?"

I had thought of this meeting in my dreams a thousand times before but never had I thought that my eyes would cheat on me so shamelessly. I could feel the tears gushing out without any inkling or a fighting chance to hold them back. I wanted to blame my 'emotion packed day' for making me so vulnerable and emotionally weak but I knew deep down that it was not anything but his presence which was so unnerving.

He offered me his handkerchief, his face devoid of any expression or feeling, as he had done so often before, when I had come to his room in tears because Maa had turned down my plea to go to Sabaa's home for her *daawat* or when Baba had issued a stern 'no' to my joining the college picnic because he did not approve of boys and girls going out together.

I kept staring at him. He was just the same the hair at his temples had grayed a little. He was wearing spectacles, his attire suave, but that was just about all. He still had the same deep brooding eyes, the same dignified gait, the same, staid and somber look on his face that could scare you if you didn't know him better. He was still my same Aditya after all these years.

A surge of tenderness overpowered me. I wanted to reach out to him, to feel him but an equally strange shyness gripped me inside. I was surprised at this new me. I recalled how I used to pull his arm dragging him out to see that stray kitten or close his eyes from behind spontaneously, how I would ruffle his hair teasingly or would write on his back to irritate him without feeling a wee bit conscious about it. How I would put my head on his shoulder while listening to my favourite Rafi songs or softly caress his face when the desire took me.

It is strange how one little ceremony round the fire had changed everything in life for me. There had been times when I wanted to scream, to ask everyone to give me a break, to see that I am still the same little girl in two pigtails, the same girl who gathered sunshine in her arms, the tinkling laughter of the moon in her eyes, who sang aloud with the birds, who whispered to the winds, who pirouetted on the rainbows and danced with the butterflies, the girl who hummed and giggled, believed and trusted, the girl who had hopes, illusions, desires, dreams.

There was so much I wanted to say to him too, so much I wanted to hear.

I simply felt that from the day I had given him my consent for the marriage, I had been living in a trance for this very moment. My life with Naveen was the price I had paid to prove my loyalty, my love, my commitment to Aditya and I hoped he knew it too.

I had paid my dues honestly, even at the cost of dying slowly inside every minute of the day. I had paid my toll when I had mutely surrendered to his command, neither protesting, nor rebelling, nor choosing a way out.

It has been agonising for me to be in a marriage where neither my heart nor my soul belonged and yet in which I was supposed to look happy and contented. I respected Naveen a lot. He was everything any woman could have ever desired, but how could I change the way my heart beat?

I wanted to share all this with Aditya. I wanted to see that same tenderness, the same love in his eyes once again, to see how deeply he had appreciated my sacrifice and my commitment. It was all that I had been blindly living for, every moment of these past years, just like an ascetic doing his penance. Today when destiny had been kind enough to send him my way, I wanted it to be that miraculous moment of my life when I could open up, all the gates of my dam within, letting my pent up emotions surge forth with full force and all my primal desires, to face him brazenly and defiantly.

I was so under the spell of my own intensity, my entire body shivering under the impact of my own emotions, my face reflecting the stark desperation of my yearnings and my eyes opening out the entire path right down to my soul for him to read me through and through.

✦

Aditya kept looking at me so strangely that it frightened me. Then suddenly as if he had drawn a curtain over his thoughts, he smiled briefly and asked, "So tell me about yourself Chutki. How have you been?"

His calling me by the playful endearment Baba would so often call me with brought back a whiff of those fragrant days, the days of carefree laughter and bliss, the days when I belonged to myself, a luxury that seemed like a fantasy now.

I tried to piece up my story, haltingly at first telling him in bits and pieces about my journey into the new world of Mrs. Bhatt that I had been forced to turn into. The unbearable agony of belonging to someone without feeling any sense of belonging. The torment of going on loving without hope, without promise, without dreams, simply because loving was the only way to be.

I told him about Baba's death, bhaiyya's marriage, Maa's ill health, my marriage which stifled me despite all the freedom and comforts, about Naveen's goodness, nobleness, which was so hugely appreciated by everyone around but which surprisingly left me untouched and homeless. As I was narrating tears flowed out heedlessly building a bridge for his love to walk right up to my wounded soul and heal me with his magic touch.

I asked timidly, "Aditya, you too must have carried me in your thoughts all these years, haven't you?"

I was so certain he would say yes.

For who could have ever loved him in his life as much as I did?

Who could have ever been devoted to him as intensely as me?

For me this conviction was not at all about being vain, it was simply about being certain of the depth of my love.

He gave me an exasperated look, "Tchh Chutki, I think you've been reading far too many romantic novels, haven't you? Come on, why would I be thinking of you all this time when I'm quite sure you must be happy and busy in your own life with Naveen?

Yes, we've been close friends. Your parents were so nice to me. But let's not weave a story out of it."

I could feel the blood pounding in my ears. Ah! The shame of it all. How coldly he had spoken, how cruelly. His words had mocked the very reason of my existence. He had besmirched everything that was beautiful and sacred to me. So we were just once-upon-a-time friends, were we? Baba and Maa had just been nice to him and he never had any reason to think of me all these years?

I hoped the earth could open up and swallow me for I dared not face him again.

Romantic novels, indeed!

✦

When the first wave of shame and anger had receded, my faith in him tried to resurface again. My belief in him was far too deep and strong to have been shaken up so easily by words. My heart refused to believe what he had so glibly spoken.

Of course he had known how I had felt about him then. I had been as transparent as daylight. He was Baba's favourite student, more like his son. Obviously Baba had trusted him to draw the consent out of me. I questioned him on all this, my voice reflecting the intensity of my hurt and disbelief as well as that unspoken desperate plea which begged him to deny his own words, just this once.

Totally unperturbed, he answered me chillingly; "I think you have a very vivid imagination. Or could be that it is a case of me being your first crush. These things happen Chutki, I don't think we need to stretch it so far. You seem to be having a fine husband and he is the stuff good husbands are made of. Not wedded to his books, papers and lectures like I am. I am really not a family man Chutki, having lived in hostels all my life. In fact emotions irritate me and really I find all these talks about love, romance quite appalling. I'm quite sure, I'd have been miserable in a marriage."

His words were like molten metal in my ears, searing me with their cynicism and ruthlessness. I was just too aghast and stunned to think straight. My eyes wide open; I looked at that stranger incredulously.

With one sweeping remark he had pulled the rug under my feet, leaving me utterly defenseless and vulnerable. I could feel myself searing under his abject rejection, my whole world blazing around me, flames of humiliation leaping up in full ferocity, shame and anguish burning my entire being in their scorching incandescence. For a moment the very reason of my being was reduced to ashes.

But love like Phoenix refuses to accept defeat, love like Phoenix rises anew from its ashes, love like Phoenix resurrects itself through its unwavering faith, indefatigable conviction and its indomitable hope.

Despite every word that he had uttered, my love surged forth with a renewed vigour, my faith held on to itself with all its might and my consciousness stood rooted firmly in the knowledge that love like ours is enduring and eternal.

And so with a fury and passion, I never knew I was capable of, I grabbed hold of his hand, put it on my head and cried, "Aditya say it now. Say it with your hand on my head that you have never loved me like a man loves his woman – deeply, intensely, and passionately. Say that you don't love me anymore. I dare you to say it Aditya. Say it if you can."

Aditya:

I was so shocked to see her sitting there, in that coupe today, all alone, looking so frail and depleted. I truly could not believe she was the same bubbly, effervescent girl with dancing eyes and a glowing face, the one I had shared a home with for four golden years of my life.

Today I came to realise the enormity of my guilt, the guilt which was killing me slowly all these years. With one consent taken with the power of my love, I had ruined her life forever.

I had thought of this meeting in my dreams a thousand times before, but never like this ever.

Oh! how I craved to hold her in my arms, to press her face to my chest and let all her pain dissolve in me forever. How I wanted to wipe away her every tear, every crease of stress, every pain and suffering from her heart. How I wanted to tell her that I had been living all these years only on the faith, that somewhere in this world she existed, smiling, happy and contented in her little new world. For sometimes just knowing that the one you love exists somewhere, becomes reason enough for you to love life.

Till I'd met Prof. Joshi.

I still cannot forget my last meeting with him. It must have been a month prior to his brain haemorrhage that I got his message asking me to come over as soon as I could. I took the very next flight to Delhi from Jaipur where I was working as an Assistant Professor in the University. He and I talked for a long time in the privacy of his study and finally when we had exchanged all trivialities, he told me he wanted to share his worries about Mrinalini. That was the first time I realised that everything was not alright with her. He confessed that he had failed her as a father. In wanting to give her what he thought was an excellent match, he had robbed her of her happiness, her dreams, her life.

He explained that on the pretext of a meeting he had gone to Lucknow and stayed with the Bhatt's for a couple of days. He could not believe that the Mrinalini he saw there was his own Chutki. Her face so listless, her eyes so dull and lifeless and her voice so distant and lost; all had been tormenting him ever since. Gone was the bounce in her steps, the twinkle in her eyes, and the chiming laughter in her voice. Instead of his earlier bundle of joy was this breathing, living corpse carrying on the duties as expected of her.

He said, "Aditya I've realised this today that neither comforts, nor goodness, nor all the nobility in the world can bring that one smile in a woman's heart, which just a moment of being in love does. I'm certain that if ever she could see her husband for the wonderful person he is, if she can ever love him as she's capable of loving; she may become our old Chutki again.

"Beta, there's nothing you and I can do for her at this stage, for I know that she would see through our efforts and resent it. But since I know you care for her, I want you to be around her, to keep an eye on her and who knows when God may grant you the opportunity to bring her out of this misery."

A month after Bhaiya called up to say that Prof. Joshi is no more. I felt completely orphaned and alone. In deference to his wishes, I applied for the post of Professor in Lucknow University.

Being in Lucknow, I thought, would give me a chance to be around her and keep an eye on her. But till today no such opportunity presented itself to me.

Today when I saw Mrinalini, all of that conversation came back to me again. On one hand, I could feel Prof. Joshi's soul reaching out to me, beseeching me to honour my oath of obedience and loyalty to my 'Guru' and on the other hand, I saw what her eyes were trying to convey. I read her intense love for me, her longings and desires. For me there could have been no greater wealth or bliss than that spontaneous offering. For me there could have been no greater joy than to tell her that I had always loved her with all my soul, with every breath in me that her love coursed through my veins every second of the day.

Yet I could not be so selfish. I had to put on an act for the sake of Prof. Joshi, I had to convince her into believing that I was a unfeeling man who had never loved her sincerely and deeply. I had to break her heart, to make her fall in love with her husband Naveen. For her own sake, I had to let her go. I knew she was heartbroken at my callousness. I knew she was crying, suffering from excruciating agony and shame. Yet, I had to cut that bond of ours which was pulling her to me incessantly. The bond she was holding on to so tenaciously that she could not touch and feel the soft, silken fibers of her new relationship with Naveen.

✦

I did it too; as God was my witness I did it to the best of my efforts. But I now realise that I had never understood Mrinalini or the depth of her love for me. Hers was the devotion of the soul, the love which transcends words, expressions, morality, life and the beyond. For someone who had the strength to sacrifice her life for me, she was not the one to be shaken up by my fake denials and false words.

When she suddenly grabbed hold of my hand, put it on her head and cried heart wrenchingly, "Aditya say it now. Say it with your hand on my head that you have never loved me like a man loves his woman – deeply, intensely, passionately. Say that you don't love me anymore. I dare you to say it Aditya. Say it if you can." I simply knew that I was defeated.

There was no way I could falsely swear on her.

I knew it then, come what may, joy or pain, life or death, seeing each other or being apart forever, I could not lie to her anymore. My love for her was far more precious than all the righteousness of life, all virtuousness, all goodness.

Every reason, every logic faded away in front of that one eternal truth.

All my defenses crumbled that very instant. All the love I had suppressed so mercilessly rushed forth brimming out uncontrollably from my eyes. Tears coursed down my cheeks unrestrained, lips quivering with a million unspoken emotions. With passion unleashed with an intensity that frightened me, I pulled her to me kissing her with a need and urgency that said it all.

I held her so close, so tightly in my grip, scared that she would vanish if I had let her go. I could feel her entire body racked with sobs. I knew those were tears of all the pent up suffering and pain, tears of relief and joy all mixed together.

I have no idea how long we stood there, it seemed like a moment, and it seemed like eternity. But slowly I loosened my grip and kissed her gently once again. I pulled her down on the berth and sitting so close that I could feel her breath, I said, "So now you know how I feel about you, my love. But Chutki that does not change anything for us, does it? My word to your father before he died still exists. Your marriage to Naveen, also does. Now you tell me my little one where do we go from here?"

She lifted up her tear drenched eyes and gazed at me with so much love and ardour that it simply took my breath away and replied, "Aditya, I understand that we are both bound by our commitments, you to Baba and me to Naveen. But it is enough for me to know that you love me for I've now realised that being drenched in love is being truly complete. Your love fills me so absolutely and completely that there is no vacuum left in me anymore. My cup runs over and I know that this love and joy will spill over on to the people around me too.

"I can now live with every situation, every hardship in life knowing that you too are there somewhere, existing in this world, that every breath I draw comes from the air that you have breathed in, that the sun that shines on me warms you too, that every evening the moonshine makes a bridge for you to walk right up to my heart softly, silently.

"Who knows what the future holds. If ever life offers us the chance, I know we'd be there for each other. But if it doesn't, then we shall still meet, beyond life. Because love outlives everything else."

I looked at her incredulously. Here was a woman in love with wisdom, that being so completely in love could only bring. Hers was a love mystic and sublime, a love that gave all of itself without any desire or expectation.

The train was moving at its full pace and I realised that it was already four thirty in the morning. Two hours to reach Lucknow. I could see Mrinalini smiling through her tears, her face next to mine, eyes looking up at me sparkling with ecstasy and bliss.

I opened the window and felt the fresh morning breeze caressing us with a promise of another day. Far away new rays of the rising sun with their golden brightness, were spreading out shyly, softly, willing to embrace the earth in their warmth and to kiss life into every nook and cranny of its erstwhile darkness.

Somehow at that moment, Rumi's words resonated in my heart –

"Out beyond ideas
of wrongdoing and rightdoing,
there is a field.

I'll meet you there
when the soul lies down
in that grass,
the world is too full to talk about,
language, ideas
– even the phrase "each other" –
do not make any sense."

✦ ✦ ✦

4

Mirages of the Heart

April 2001:

Innocence embraces the whole world as its own. Just as the fresh morning breeze caresses the entire earth. Just as the pristine dew drops fall equally on the tree tops and the grass blades. And just as a little bird sings for everyone around it.

Minni had two pigtails and dancing eyes. For her the whole length and breadth of Durga Marg was home. There wasn't a house she would think twice before walking in with full proprietory airs. She knew exactly when Sharma aunty watched her afternoon repeat show of CID, when Anjali aunty sat down for her pooja, or when Tanisha's mummy took her afternoon nap every day. Minni was all of five and extremely proud of it. A one child entertainment show, she could keep her audience regaled for hours together. Sudha, her mother, would often admonish her for being such a chatterbox. Sudha was of the firm opinion that it was not at all becoming of girls to be such babblers, but Minni's Baba Madhukar would immediately stand up to her defense and after an argument which would ensue for an hour or so the matter would invariably be adjourned for another day.

Madhukar worked in a leading refrigerator company as a Branch Manager and lived in his parental house in Jaipur. His wife, Sudha, had been a school teacher before marriage, but her wedding to Madhukar and then Minni's arrival soon after followed by the birth of Ankur (who was now five months old) never gave her the leisure to apply again. Her small family, especially her two highly demanding kids, were more than enough to keep her occupied the whole day long. Many a times she would crib that all the house-work, shopping for the daily grocery, nursing of their new-born, drained her out completely leaving not an ounce of energy to run after his little darling who'd suddenly take it upon herself to give her favourite Sonia Aunty a surprise visit simply because the mood took her so.

So often would she tell Madhukar, "I wish Ija could come over and stay with us for at least a few months. This is the only time when one needs someone experienced and responsible at home. Minni will go to her new school from this July, Ankur will start teething any day now and you are always on tours nowadays. How can you expect me to manage everything alone?"

Madhukar would mumble, "Well what do you expect me to do? I do have to earn the salary also. You know I had asked Ija to come, but if she did not leave the hills for *Bauji*, do you think she'd come now? And anyway, this is the time for *Dhaan* plantation in hills. There's no way I can ask her to come."

Minni would wonder why grown-ups were so worried always. Why was her Maa always working and so tense? Why couldn't she be more like Sonia Aunty who wore the prettiest dresses Minni had ever seen, who always smelt so wonderful that one wanted to hug her and who always had time to talk to Minni and sing those lovely nursery rhymes to her, no matter when she came.

Minni would always sit and ponder over such serious issues of life, by the big window of their living room especially when Sudha forbade her to step out of the house or when she asked her to be a big girl and keep an eye on Ankur who was always sleeping anyways. Minni would wonder how anyone could sleep so much! She was quite sure she couldn't have been half as sleepy when she was Ankur's age.

Minni loved to sit by that window. From here she could watch people going on about their various jobs, like the vendors with their attractive wares calling out to the housewives. She could see maids in bright ghagra cholis rushing to their work. In the afternoons they would sit under the shade of that big neem tree and open out their boxes wrapped in colourful scarves, giggling and chatting as they devoured their meals which looked so appetising to Minni from afar. Sometimes sparrows would come and sit on the branches so close by that she could reach out and touch them if she wanted to. She loved watching squirrels frisking around, chasing each other and looking at her with beady thoughtful eyes. At least it was much better than playing with those same old toys over and over again. Sometimes she wished Ankur could've been a little bigger so that she could play with him and tell him all about her play school which was just across the road although Maa had said that she would be going to a much bigger and smarter school from this July.

It was during one such introspection by her window one late afternoon that Minni saw Anandi *Mami* for the first time. She was walking into their drive with Vinod *da,* Maa's cousin and a very frequent visitor to their house. Dressed in a bright purple sari, she had a big red bindi on her forehead, the size of a two rupee coin that Baba had given her one day and which she had kept in the wooden box that stored all her treasures. She was elderly though not very old, fair, pleasantly plump and had the liveliest face that Minni had ever seen. It was a Sunday morning and Madhukar was reading the newspaper in the verandah on his favourite cane chair. After a lot of cheerful pleasantries and Maa calling Minni to the kitchen to help her carry savouries outside to the visitors, they all settled down to serious conversation. Minni kept hovering around, curious about this new guest who had a voice at times like a cascade falling down on stones making tinkling sounds and at times like a river rushing forward; whooshing, gurgling, swirling sounds varying with the hues of her conversation. She appeared so vibrant and colourful both in her manner and speech that Minni was instinctively drawn towards her and had this strange impulse to touch her and see if she was for real. As if she could sense her unexpressed thoughts, Anandi Mami pulled Minni over to herself ever so warmly, "Well, now look at my little doll. Isn't she adorable?" And without any more ado she was swiftly plonked onto to her soft, cuddly lap with plump, satin arms around her. Although shy, Minni loved being where she had been deposited so promptly. The lap smelled of fresh jasmine and despite all strangeness felt very familiar.

Minni could see that the elders were too wrapped up in their discussion to notice her. Vinod da was quite agitated,

"Mami all your life you slaved for those sons of yours. You skimped, saved, made their careers, got them married, raised their children while they worked and made money.

"Twenty years back, when Mama had retired from service and you were required to vacate the government quarters, with practically no money in the bank, these very sons, refused to give you shelter under the pretext that there was not enough space in their house, for two more people. Space? My foot. How is it Mami that these people have space in their house, for their children, their wife and even a full time maid if needed; but they never have space for their parents? Shame on them.

It was so nice of your brother then, to insist on your coming and making your home with him. I know you went there only on condition that he would accept at least a basic amount from you, by way of rent, failing which you would not step into his house. The arrangement had worked out perfectly so far, but now I believe after the sad demise of your brother, his children are selling off that house and you have decided to look for a new accommodation on rent. The more I think of this, the more disgusted I am with your sons. Do they really have no sensitivity, no humanity, no gratefulness, no conscience? How stone-hearted can they be to be so unmoved by your plight?

Minni could see mami wiping a stray tear from her cheek. Madhukar retorted, "Vinod da, it's happening everywhere now. Let's not make her more upset over it. But I agree she should not live with them now, even if they ask her to. She can easily find an accommodation for the two of them. Mama's pension may not be large, but it should suffice for their needs, and by God's grace they both are in good health too. Let her sons realise their mistake and feel sorry. Then maybe mama and she can think about shifting in with them."

Vinod da seemed to agree with this which turned the conversation to the possibilities of a new accommodation for the two of them. Minni heard her Baba saying, "Vinod da the trouble is that people don't rent their house to retired people nowadays, no matter how much we convince the owner of their character and goodness. A landlord today would want to give his house on a company lease. It spells security for him you see."

The conversation went on and on till Anandi Mami realising that it was nearly lunch time, got worried about mama at home and insisted on leaving. Madhukar and Sudha promised to think of some possible accommodations for her, to check out some 'To let' notices around and get back to Vinod da as soon as possible.

That night lying in her small cot near Maa and Baba, Minni could hear them going over Anandi mami's visit in the morning. Sudha seemed extremely upset, "Is that why parents sacrifice everything for their children? So that when they are old and weak, their children can neglect them and throw them out, to the mercy of Gods? Ah it's sad. Listen can we not find them a good accommodation nearby? They both could do with some company and really mami is so sweet. Didn't you see how she loved our Minni?"

Madhukar who was mulling over various possibilities suddenly said, "Sudha, why don't we ask them to shift into our two room set that we'd kept aside for Ija all this while. I'm sure they won't be able to rent a house in any case. It's impossible to secure a home on personal lease, especially if you are a retired couple. Our set might be a little small for them, but look at the security and company they'll have. As for us, we know that they are people of high principles. A little rent won't do us any harm and you can also have the comfort of having an experienced and responsible relative close by to give you a hand in times of emergency and need."

The more they talked the more the idea jelled for them and Minni felt a surge of thrill and excitement coursing through her veins despite her drooping eyes which were refusing to stay open any longer.

And so one fine day with all details settled out, with mama and mami convinced that this one option was truly God sent for them, they finally moved into Minni's home, albeit a little diffidently and shyly, weighed down by the knowledge that the rent being asked of them was just a façade to maintain the pretense that it was a commercial transaction.

For Minni it was the most exciting event of her entire life. She kept watching the small tempo unloading Anandi mami's belongings, the iron trunks, likes of which she had never seen before, a small wooden temple with a big dome on top, utensils that could feed an army, huge woks and ladles which were so strange to look at, two charpoys and a couple of jute *mudahs*, a small TV which looked like it belonged to another era...

Minni kept dancing around mami who was working along with the two men unloading their meager belongings checking if everything had arrived just as dispatched. And when Minni queried, "But mami, how will you put all this in those two rooms?," she laughed and answered, "Oh, I've a *jaadoo ki chhadee* with me. You just wait, it'll all disappear in corners you'll never know." Minni's eyes popped out with excitement.

Oh, what fun! Mami sure looked like an angel and now to find out that she had a wand too. This was absolutely amazing.

Soon Sudha called them over for lunch and all the excitement was forgotten. After lunch mami went back to her unpacking and Minni was ordered to sleep with Ankur since the days were getting hot. By the evening when she ran back to mami's rooms, she was stunned to see the whole room looking like a pretty painting and sure as anything all the belongings had disappeared into corners she couldn't see. Oh, to have missed looking at the wand, but mami so sweetly hugged and comforted her, promising that she would definitely show it to her some other day, which brought laughter back into her disappointed eyes.

In no time mami had settled down to her normal life and activities. Her walking into their little world definitely looked like magic to Minni. It was as if she'd touched her wand and transformed their mundane lives altogether. She brought in laughter and words into their silent routines, filling everything around her with colour and life. Everyday Minni would be woken up by her melodious chantings of *Namaamii shameeshaan nirvaan roopam* or *Om shuklaambhar dharam vishnum shashi varnam chaturbhujam* with the wafting fragrance of incense sticks and jasmine flowers all mixed up together, so mesmerising that it pulled at her chords irresistibly. Taking her bath as fast as she could, so that mami would let her ring the hand bell and offer the flowers after the aarti, she would rush over to their rooms with wings on her feet. After the aarti there was an added temptation of the Prasad which would be a sweet confection like *Singhal-puas* which would be as soft as butter, fresh coconut laddus or halwah; whichever, in mami's words, *Bhagwaan ji* would tell her to make that day.

After her pooja mami would come over and take charge of Ankur leaving Sudha free to attend to her kitchen. It was very obvious that she really loved children. She would often tell Minni about her five grandchildren all of whom she had brought up single-handedly, till they were around five years old, and how none of them ever had to be taken to those stupid hospitals and silly doctors, who did not know a thing about children anyways.

This would often leave Minni rolling into peals of laughter, for no one she ever knew dared to call the doctors silly. But mami was mami and she could get away with anything. Moreover she was a real genie and the crankiest child would settle in her arms as quietly as a happy kitten with not so much as a whimper, which was a feat very few women could challenge. Ankur gurgled and giggled in her hands, dimpling into his lovely cherubic smile that tickled Minni's heart. Mami would spread out a *dhurrie* on the floor and put Ankur down on it proceeding to massage him leisurely for an hour or so cooing and singing to him. Then she would move his limbs all around, to make him strong and flexible as she said. She would finally end it up with a bath and then hand him over to Sudha to feed him. By the end of this entire exercise Ankur would go off to sleep feeling fresh and light and would not wake up till after a few hours.

Mami was equally wonderful in the kitchen too. Very often Minni would be drawn into her little kitchen by the tempting aromas of her cooking and slowly over the days she'd end up eating more of her meals there, than in her Maa's kitchen. Sudha too, often confessed to Madhukar that mami was truly so gifted that she could churn out delicacies with every day's ordinary ingredients, like raw bananas, bottle gourd, coconut kernels and jackfruit. Her cooking was the most effortless thing that could be. She just had the gift of flavour in her hands and no matter what she added or threw into her work instinctively it simply ended up turning out into the tastiest dish ever. Had she even wanted, she couldn't have given anyone a recipe of her dishes, for truly there were none. But more endearing than her cooking, was the warmth and love with which she fed everyone. Sudha remarked that you could actually watch her relishing your enjoyment and pleasure in her cooking. And this was what satiated you above all.

Sudha loved the way mami cooked the crispiest, flakiest paratha and then squashed it in between her palms, burning hot as it were, before serving it.

She could also churn out great desserts in a jiffy from whatever was available in the kitchen without much ado.

June 2001:

Minni witnessed a sea change in her mother over the past months. She appeared more relaxed and much happier. There were no more complaints to Baba about his going away on tours, about being burdened with all the household chores and the kids. Mami was with her like a Rock of Gibraltar, always around and so dependable.

The days had become longer and Madhukar ordered two Khus Khus curtains, one for their home and the other for Mami's bedroom. Minni loved the earthy smell that wafted out of those curtains when they sprinkled water on it in the hot afternoons. Mami was delighted with this unexpected gift and convinced Sudha to let Minni take her midday nap with them after the meals. This new arrangement proved to be a great relief for Sudha as much as it was a blessing for Minni. Cuddled up in the softness of the quintessential mother in mami, blissful in her jasmine fragrance, in the cooled and darkened room; Minni would be transported to innumerable tales of wonderland through that deeply soothing magic of her voice. Floating on the waves of slumber, she would sail off to unknown times and lands and meet scary devils and handsome princes and flying horses and magic lamps.

It was finally when Sonia and Mrs. Sharma remarked that not having seen Minni for over a month they had been quite worried about her; that Sudha realised how there had been a complete transformation in Minni's life by the coming of mami into their world.

While all was going great for Minni, it was just the opposite with Ankur. He had become crankier over the past days. He was running a slight temperature and had lost his appetite too. Noticing Sudha's increasing stress and worry, mami gave her some homeopathic medicines asking her to postpone the idea of visiting a regular doctor for about a week and to try out these sweet pills for that period. After just about four days, Ankur was back to normal, grinning and rolling on the mat like a happy puppy all over again. It was then that mami gleefully confessed she had been able to make out that those were teething symptoms and as his gums were swollen too; she had given him calcium and iron pills.

Sudha was overcome with gratitude and joy and thus the days passed on with mami becoming deeply entrenched into their lives, their troubles and joys getting interwoven with one another in many more ways than one.

As for mama, he was a saint at heart, as Madhukar had often declared to Sudha when alone. A deeply spiritual man and a scholar at heart, his day would start very early with yoga and prayers. He would go for his walks, come back and tend to the garden as both Madhukar and Sudha were hard pressed for time. After which he would quietly and leisurely read his papers over the breakfast. His entire day went into reading, prayers, introspection and doing odd jobs in the house. All the conversation that ever got done in that home came from mami, whereas mama just always smiled and kept mum. It was a queer marriage of two souls that were chalk and cheese and yet were deep down fused into each other.

In the meantime Vinod da came and went as usual once a fortnight, although both Sudha and Madhukar observed that there was a sudden escalation in his attention for mami. Sometimes he would get a bunch of bananas for her or sometimes a box of puas that his wife had made that day and he would continuously impress upon mami how much he worried about her welfare.

Very soon, he announced that he would be holding a *Satyanarayan Puja* in his house and requested mami to come over and take charge of all the arrangements. He pleaded, "In the absence of my parents, mama and you are the eldest of the family and no one can hold a torch to you when it comes to rituals and ceremonies. Mami, I'm banking on you to see this through, please."

Simple soul that she was, mami was so overcome by Vinod da's speech that she couldn't stop dabbing her eyes for hours together. Overwhelmed and moved beyond words, deeply touched at being considered the eldest of the family, she took it as a personal challenge to make that puja a success. Everything that would be needed was noted down, mama was asked to get the step ladder and bring down the large wok and ladles from the loft along with a couple of large vessels and jugs. After all as elders it was their duty to think of everything. She also took out the homemade ghee that she had saved over the months for making prasad. "Oh, you simply can't trust the ghee sold in the market nowadays," she said with a big sigh and then proceeded to inform with a subtle pride in her voice that hers was absolutely pure and untouched by any other hand. She had laid out two saris for herself. "This one I'd wear in the morning. As the eldest lady of the family, I must be there before anyone else. There would be innumerable chores to be seen to. I'll have to cook the prasad, see to the sitting arrangement, decorate the temple and keep everything ready for the pandit ji. It's so improper when senior members themselves come late or are more concerned about their looks than the work in the home." Mami's excitement knew no bounds and neither Sudha nor Madhukar had the heart to puncture her joy.

On the day of the puja, mami left for Vinod da's home on a rickshaw, worried and excited, with Minni along for company while holding on to wok and vessels, ladles and jugs, the huge pot of ghee and that extra sari to wear for the function.

Once there Minni saw a different mami altogether. She went straight to the kitchen and arranged her pots and vessels, took a rapid inventory and started cleaning, cutting, chopping all vegetables and in no time tempting aromas of different dishes were attacking Minni's hunger unmercifully. She then cleaned and washed a separate area where she prepared the special prasad of *Kasaar* and *Roti* and *kheer*. Once she was through with this, she cleaned the temple floor and painted it with the red *Geru* and then drew out intricate designs with white rice paste using the finger tips of her right hand. Vinod da kept hovering around, admiring her art, all the while praising how truly complicated it was and how very few could make these *Aipans* now. Then the temple was decorated, all diyas and puja items kept ready just so. The Prasad, with a few tulsi leaves placed on it, was duly covered with foil and flowers arranged perfectly too. She had got a tiny banana plant from the house, "I know how impossible it is to procure these small yet essential items at the last minute. And can you ever imagine a Satyanarayan puja without a banana tree?"

Vinod da looked mighty thrilled with her attention for details and planning. Addressing his wife he declared grandiosely, "There's just no way we can ever match our elders despite our education, exposure and smartness. For theirs' is the wisdom and experience gained by years of tough living and working single-handedly." Minni observed that mami had blushed deep red at such an open demonstration of admiration and regards and she was soon working again with an added fervour.

By the time she was giving her last touches, pandit ji had arrived. Hard pressed for time, he asked everyone to sit down immediately, for the puja had to start exactly at the auspicious moment. Mami wanted so much to change into that lovely orange sari she had specially bought for the occasion, but as she later said, "After all as an elder of the family, it was my duty to see that the puja starts at the right time." And so it was performed with everyone looking nice and bright except for mami; who was looking disheveled with her faded cotton sari that had marks of turmeric and geru sprinkled over it and smell of food and sweat all over.

When the photos were being clicked, no one called out to her and mama (who had come just before the puja with Madhukar and Sudha). Mami was oblivious to all this, glorifying in the satisfaction that she'd pulled the feat off in the end.

The event over they all returned home together. Vinod da gave his perfunctory thanks to mama and mami and the evening was considered as closed, except for Sudha. She was extremely upset at what she later complained to Madhukar was 'downright crafty and selfish of Vinod da'; but on the face of it, looking at mami's glowing face, she thought it prudent to remain silent.

And as they had anticipated Vinod da's visits petered out in the next few months owing to a sudden and excessive load of work.

Sometimes a very small incident can open up a 'pandora's box' of events in our lives. So it happened with mami too. Mami suddenly became the most sought after person in the small Kumaoni community, a community comprising of people connected and inter connected with each other. Every other day there would be someone at her side of the house with half a dozen bananas or a quarter kilo of *Rautela's Baal mithaai* expressing his delight at having been fortunate enough to learn about her whereabouts and his hitherto unknown relationship with such a close relative and then in the subsequent meeting requesting her to come over to his puja of *Naamkaran* or *Annapraashan* or *Grihpravesh*. That being invited entailed assuming responsibility of all important duties, was something that was never spelt out but always true.

Mami was always ready to work her bones out for anyone who requested her, without any desire for name, good will or material benefits. This would often annoy Sudha and she would want to shake her up to see the truth for what it was.

September 2001:

Life had suddenly shifted to a higher gear over the last two months. Minni was now a big girl, or so she insisted as she had started going to a proper school which was frightening at first, but so much more wonderful now. It was a big school with an imposing building and large lawns and Minni who was too scared earlier to even walk through its gate, now felt a huge sense of pride just by looking at it. It was mama who quietly volunteered to drop and pick her up from her bus stop everyday and although they were both very awkward with each other in the beginning. Minni's spontaneity and liveliness bridged the chasm between them. Just a week of walking up to the bus stop and waiting for the bus had turned them into the thickest of friends and in about a month mama found himself learning all about 'Paper Fortune Teller', 'Rock, Paper, Scissors', 'Stepu', 'Tippy Tippy Top' and all the other games that he never knew existed under the vast blue sky.

Minni's world was unfurling out in all its excitement and joy with new friends, new teachers and still newer activities. Mami's role in her life was still very important, but she wasn't the fulcrum anymore although mami with all her wisdom welcomed this change contentedly.

And then one day Minni came back from school to find inviting aromas coming over from mami's kitchen. As she peeped in she saw a much excited mami dressed in her crispy colourful albeit old sari, arranging some flower stems in a make-shift vase. Beaming from ear to ear she said, "Guess who's coming today Minni? My son, Naresh. Oh, I knew he'd come one day. Can a child ever forget his mother? No way baba, no way!

Your mama, Oh, what does he know about children? One does not know everything just by reading a few books.

See, I have made his favourite *aaloo ka gutuka* and *kheer* and *besan ka laddoo*. You must see how he loves my cooking. No one, he says, no one can make kheer like his Ija. Come over in the evening Minni, then you can see my boy."

Minni was eaten up with curiosity for the one who was so dear and special to mami. She would have given anything to have a look at him but for the coincidence that Madhukar decided to take his family out for a long overdue shopping that very evening. However, she didn't have to wait very long for getting more news as mami came charging over first thing next morning, bursting with excitement at having had a wonderful reunion with her first born, the apple of her eyes. She was besides herself with joy recounting all that had transpired the evening before. Starting from how impressive her son looked in his new big car "so spacious that it could've taken all of us in and yet have as much space left", to how much he said he had missed her and bauji and wished they all could be together again like old times, to his enchanting confession that there was still no one, who could make kheer half as delicious as that of his Ija's, to a hundred other such remarkable details.

Mami's face was suffused with a deep pink which conveyed her exhilaration and a glow that was simply celestial. She had got a bowl of her homemade laddoos and thrusting it into Sudha's hands she nearly screamed in delight, "Sudha I wanted you to be the first one to know that my granddaughter's marriage has been fixed for the next month. The family is one of the leading industrial groups of our country. They have big businesses all over but they are still humble and traditional people. They are insisting on a very simple, traditional wedding. Isn't my granddaughter lucky?"

Sudha expressed every bit of pleasure that such news merited and also marvelled at how perfect her laddoos had turned out to be. No wonder her son couldn't appreciate anyone else's cooking, she teased. Mami blushed so endearingly that Sudha hugged her with all her warmth.

Now that the ice was broken, her son was often seen visiting his mother more under the guise of, "This house is on way to my new project and since I was going by this road, I thought I might as well meet you too." And just as naturally mami would keep something or the other of his choice cooked for him and serve it under a similar guise of, "Oh, I made this today. But you know me; I always end up cooking more than required. So now there's enough for you to eat too?"

But what was extremely strange was mama's indifference to this reunion. It was as if his general aloofness and detachment in life had extended to the people around him too. This would tear mami's heart out. She'd often complain about it to Sudha saying, "My poor boy, it bleeds my heart to see him so dejected. I swear he makes every effort to talk to his bauji. But His Holiness is too involved in himself to bother about his own blood and bones." Not being able to continue, she would often lapse into a melancholic silence, her eyes reflecting the hurt deep within, much to Minni's distress. It would often make her wonder how could such a wonderful mama, who never uttered a harsh word, who laughed so much with her; ever make such a sweet mami so upset?

Mami was indeed very childlike and spontaneous. Her emotions flashed across her face with an innocence which belied her age. And much as she was miffed with mama's heartlessness towards their son's efforts, she couldn't suppress her elation at the impending wedding of her first grandchild. Every day she would come up, armed with the latest news that she had gathered from Naresh, her son, on the prospective wedding, "Oh Sudha, Naresh says that its going to be the grandest wedding the Kumaoni community has ever seen. Naresh wants to do everything in the most traditional way, just as the groom's family has desired. He wants me to personally handle the *Suwal Pathai* and the *Rangwali* for the wedding."

A few days later she was brimming with, "Sudha the groom's family will be holding the reception of the wedding in their Nainital Resorts. Naresh says that the place is like a dreamland, on the top of the mountains, overlooking the Naini Lake." She giggled happily and continued." He says that after the reception they've requested us to stay there for another week as their guest. He says you and bauji have never been out on a vacation as you were so busy taking care of our needs. Now God has given me this opportunity to take you both for a vacation. In fact he wants to make this a yearly ritual from now on.

"He's such a loving boy, my Naresh. And is so worried about his bauji. He says that once this wedding is over, he's going to take bauji for a full check up in one of those multi-specialty hospitals. He doesn't care how much money he has to spend just as long as his bauji keeps hale and hearty."

And then the next day she'd come up with, "Preeti his daughter is getting her nose pierced today, as her in-laws want her to wear their heirloom *nath*, nose ring which was worn by the groom's great grandmother, his grandmother, and finally his mother."

"Naresh wants me to make the *aipun* for the *Dhuliargh*. He's really taking so much pains over his daughter's wedding."

And thus everyday there was so much that Sudha and Madhukar learnt about this imminent grand marriage, about Naresh – what a responsible man he has turned out to be, how much he cares. It's just that the poor boy does not believe in open demonstration of his affections, thereby getting misunderstood by everyone. How he appreciates every little thing about his mother, also what mami thought that mama and she should be doing for Naresh. After all what are parents for if not to guide, manage work and share the benefits of their long experience in such events?

October 2001:

It's so surprising how just a little attention, a little time can transform the entire world of elderly parents and infuse a new life into their ageing limbs. The next few days Minni saw a totally rejuvenated mami stitching falls on new saris that, she said, belonged to her granddaughter's trousseau. Very smugly she declared, "As if I'll allow any stupid seamstress to fleece my son of his hard earned money for a job that I could so easily do in my lazy afternoons. Now I don't have to waste my time sleeping as I did earlier."

One day she saw mami dragging out her old iron trunks and removing the dried neem leaves, naphthalene balls which had been reduced to half their size and the outer layer of the cotton sari which had kept the contents inside wrapped up till then. Reverently she pulled out the purest of silk saris, the original genuine brocade, gauzy tissues, intricately embroidered Banarasi silk and the pure Tibetean brocade. All of these belonged to her mother who came from a royal family, she informed Minni. She opened and examined them one by one, finally choosing two saris which Minni thought looked heavenly. Mami told her that these were for her Preeti as she would be a bride very soon. From the rest she chose the ones with the most beautiful borders and pallus. These she removed mercilessly so that they could be used elsewhere by the bride.

Many a time Minni would find her cleaning, roasting and grinding masalas in her kitchen and noticing her surprise she would say, "Minni, it's my grand daughter's wedding and these are the things we do when we have a marriage in our home. You know I only trust my spices for cooking and that's why my food tastes better."

She would collect all her home cooked ghee, pickles in fresh jars. It's all for the wedding she would say.

However, one day when Sudha took a jar of freshly made lime pickle for her, she found mami crumpled on the ground, looking piteously forlorn. After much cajoling she confided that mama had categorically told her that he cannot spare any money for the gift of jewellery for their granddaughter. She spoke in a whisper, "All my life I've lived, as he wanted me to, not questioning, not complaining, accepting his wish as my command. And now once, just once when I expressed a small wish; he turned that down too!

Just think of it, we are the grandparents of the bride. When every single relative will ask what has the grandmother given; what will my son say – Saris!

Oh, the very idea is so embarrassing. I don't even feel like going for the wedding.

But my poor child. He's banking on me to see him through this ordeal. How can I let him down? Oh why is your mama so difficult? All these men are so heartless, so cruel."

It required all of Sudha's tact and skill along with a number of real and imaginary parallels, to convince mami that it wasn't just mama but the entire masculine race which was insensitive and incapable of appreciating relationships, expectations and one's desire to honour them. But in the end she did have a much calmer and composed mami racking her brains for any possible solution to this quandary.

The solution revealed itself through her twinkling eyes brimming with mischief, two days later. She asked Sudha in a hushed voice, "Sudha, I don't know what are the latest trends in jewellery but I think you would have some idea. Listen do you think this would be a suitable gift for my Preeti?" Saying this she opened her closed palms to reveal a heavy bracelet of gold, with the strangest sheen of yellow that Sudha and Minni had ever seen. "Oh mami," whispered Sudha in a voice full of reverence and awe, "This is simply divine." Mami blushed a soft pink. "Isn't it?" She said "It is pure 24 carat gold. You know my father was the Deewan of His Highness General Maharaja Sir Ganga Singh ji of Bikaner in 1920s. This was a gift given to him by Maharaja himself for his loyalty. This is a part of couple of pieces I've kept with me because of its sentimental value. All the rest of my meagre jewellery I'd divided long back between my two daughters-in-law."

Much later in the night Minni overheard Sudha telling Madhukar "I wonder if mami is not being too reckless." Madhukar retorted, "Come on Sudha, its her personal matter. Let's not get too involved, OK."

Having found her gift, mami sat down to stitch a beautiful *Zaardozi batua* to offer the gift in and Minni kept hovering around her handing her out the pearls and beads as instructed each time. For Minni's enthusiasm and efforts mami personally stitched her the prettiest lehnga in deep pink with golden motifs and border, from one of her old silk saris, to be worn on the wedding day.

Then it was mami's turn to open her trunk of saris. She called Sudha over to help her decide what to wear on the day of Ganesh puja, on Sangeet, on marriage and then for the reception too. She quivered nervously, "Sudha I don't want them to be ashamed of me. But really I just have these simple silk saris. The few heavy brocade saris that I possess, would truly make me look ridiculous. So do you think these will do for the resort? There'll be so many distinguished guests and I don't want them to think less of my Preeti or Naresh because of my shabbiness."

Sudha convinced her that with her looks and carriage no one could think of her as anything but royalty and that she would look like a queen even in the simplest cotton sari. But still they rummaged through the entire lot and selected the best saris out of them for various occasions.

Mami however was still very skeptical if mama would finally agree to go with them for the reception and the extended holiday, for mama had taken to getting all clamped up at the very talk of Naresh and the wedding. Sudha however convinced mami that this was all a phase and he would come round during the actual occasion. There was no way mama would grudge mami her one time happiness.

It was Diwali on the 20th and everyone plunged into it with great gusto. For Sudha and Madhukar it held an added significance as it was Ankur's first Diwali. Appreciating the importance of the same, mami stitched a lovely red dress with a golden border for Ankur, from one of her old silk sari and from the rest of it, she stitched an equally lovely frock for Minni. The five days of Diwali starting from *Dhanteres, Chhoti Diwali, Lakshmi Pujan* or *Diwali, Govardhan puja* to *Bhaiyya Duj* were all celebrated with full fervour and gaiety. Naresh called on mami, mama, Madhukar and Sudha with sweets and even brought some fire crackers for Minni, the kinds which gave out lovely multicoloured sparkles and fumes.

Ever since the last week of October there had been a great sense of urgency in mami's demeanour. As the wedding day drew nearer mami's excitement grew by leaps and bounds, spilling over in her words that cascaded out of her incessantly: 'There couldn't be a son more loving than my Naresh. He says he'll be sending his car for me every morning. He wanted both of us to shift there at least for ten days, but you know your mama ji. He says he's very happy where he is and he'd thank everyone to leave him alone.'

Or 'Oh, there's so much work to be done Sudha. Today I cleaned their kitchen, their puja room and arranged all the provisions along with my spices for the wedding.'

Or 'Today I made tins and tins of savouries and tomorrow I'll be making sweets for the whole day.'

Minni who followed mami like a little lamb noticed that mami would be too tired in the night to eat anything and would sleep off without her dinner. Her ankles and feet would be swollen up, which she confided in Minni, was because of her standing up for long hours in the kitchen. She would get up early, cook mama's lunch and dinner and then leave as soon as the car honked at the gate.

November 2001:

The first blush of winter was creeping in softly and gently, flirting with the somber and staid days of warm autumn. One could feel that little nip in the morning air and in the evenings and could see that subtle hint of fog. It was an incredibly pleasant weather with a feeling of festivity flowing deep within, even though all the major festivals were over. The wedding which was scheduled for Sunday the fourth of November, promised to be a huge success, considering all the efforts and the detailing that had gone into it.

The day before the wedding was the *Ganesh puja;* prayers invoking Lord Ganesha whose divine grace dispels all evils and promotes a successful and peaceful completion of the ceremony. Mami was dressed up and ready, early in the morning. She had decided to take Minni along with her so that she could also enjoy the fun and festivities of the marriage ceremonies. As they approached the wedding house, Minni gave out a gasp in sheer amazement. The house had been decorated with strings and strings of sparkling lights draped on all its sides from the rooftop to the windows on the ground floor. The entire boundary wall was covered with braids of lovely thick marigold flowers of the colour of the rising winter sun. The trees inside and outside the boundary were adorned with twinkling fairy lights of deep blue and red colors. Even at that time of the morning the overall impact of this beauty was bewitching. To Minni it looked like a house straight out from a fairytale.

Once inside, mami handed Minni over to a group of children of her age and like it happens everywhere with young children, it didn't take them long to be the thickest of friends. They all played the same kinds of games and so very soon they were actively involved in the intricacies of their sport. Minni loved running around in the big backyard with her new found friends but would peep in and check out on mami from time to time.

Mami had started off the day by decorating the entire temple with strings of jasmine, roses and marigold flowers. She had then decorated the entire floor of the temple with the traditional aipun, the special *chowkis* which only she could paint so intricately and so fast. Following this, she had checked and cross checked every item required by the pandit ji for the puja. Every little lamp was kept ready with the wick and ghee, every requirement right at hand. Once satisfied she took charge of the Kitchen where Minni later found her busy cooking huge vessels of confection and savouries for the puja-prasad and lunch.

Meanwhile the puja had started. Naresh his family, mami's younger son Suresh and his family and other relatives had all congregated dressed in their new outfits, glittering and shimmering and merrily chatting away. Minni kept looking out for mami, but she was still busy preparing the feast for the entire family with a couple of unskilled helpers in the kitchen. She however came out a couple of times when pandit ji needed to consult her regarding some ritual or the other.

After the puja, mami got together some other married ladies, most of them a little elderly and they were soon singing traditional songs and rolling out round *papads* of flour. Minni and her gang tired after running around, sat down and watched them in great fascination. Mami told them that these were *Suwales* and would be fried and sent in a basket along with sweets and dry fruits to the grooms house.

Then the ladies made two dolls *Samadhi* and *Samadhan* – ather and mother of the groom out of flour, rice, sesame and jaggery, giggling away all the time. And very mischievously they put a hat on the Samdhi's head, a cigarette on his lips, a pair of shades and so on. To the doll that would represent the samdhan they added a nath, a fancy hair pin and a necklace among other things. It all seemed fun and games to Minni.

Once this was completed, they took out a Harmonium and a Dholak and it was then that Minni overheard some of the ladies saying that there was no one around who could beat Anandi mami in playing the dholak and singing traditional marriage songs. For the next two hours mami built up a mood and a tempo which was simply amazing. She had a lovely yet powerful voice and the number of songs she remembered outnumbered everyone else's. So many young girls and ladies couldn't help jumping up dancing to her beats. While all this was going on, the Mehndiwali was adorning the bride's hands and feet with intricate and elaborate designs of mehndi. Her assistants were busy decorating the palms of all the young married and unmarried women in the function.

Later when they were about to go home, Naresh put his arm around mami and said smilingly, "You've already made this marriage a success Ija. I don't think anyone will forget Preeti's sangeet for months to come. By the way there's a cocktail party and 'formal sangeet' with the DJ in the night, but I know you won't be interested in such functions, so I did not invite you." Mami who was really too tired said, "Yes, you are so right Naresh and your bauji are all alone in the house. So I have to go anyways."

Minni somehow wished they could've seen that dance function too but she was a sweet and loving child and knew that mami needed to rest after all that work. So the car drove them back in the evening.

The next day Minni woke up with a wooly feeling of excitement in her stomach. Today was that big day for which they had waited so long. She kept thinking of that dreamlike pretty pink lehnga that mami had stitched for her and was now hanging in her mother's wardrobe. Sudha had bought her pink and golden bangles and a golden necklace to go with the lehnga. Finally she would be wearing them all today.

She coaxed Sudha to get her ready as fast as possible. Sudha dressed her up in her red silk frock with the golden border, the one which mami had stitched her for Diwali. The lehnga she was told would be given to her in the evening, just before the marriage ceremonies.

The car arrived on time and they reached the wedding house just when everyone there was waking up to their morning cups of tea. Mami again entered the kitchen and got down to getting the breakfast ready for the entire family and their relatives. Minni hovered around her as her yesterday's group of friends was still not ready. After a couple of hours pandit ji arrived and a fresh round of puja was done. It was then announced that mami, Naresh and his wife would be keeping a fast, with no food and water for the whole day so that they could do the kanyadaan in the night.

Soon after, the groom's sisters and sisters-in-law arrived with *ubtan* which had already been used by the groom before his bath. This paste was then applied to Preeti by all married ladies present there and the bride was asked to take her bath.

To Minni all this appeared so strange and exciting. She also marvelled at the fact that her mami was such an expert in everything. The day thus continued with full preparations for the wedding in the evening. Mami once again got busy preparing a whole feast for all in the house.

In the evening Sudha, Madhukar and mama came and stayed for as long as the *kanyadaan* which took place just before the midnight. And then, since it was getting very late and cold and since both Ankur and mama needed to sleep; they took their leave. Minni too was asked to accompany them.

Mami however had to stay back, as she had to cook the traditional singhal-puas and aaloo ka gutuka for the early morning breakfast for the groom's family.

She came back home by noon, on 5th Monday the next day, too weak and tired after a full day's fast and all the running around, cooking and singing. She informed Sudha that the reception was scheduled for Thursday, the 8th of November and she had heard Naresh giving instructions to everyone at home to be ready to leave for Nainital on Wednesday early morning. The cars would be ready and they should not want to be delayed by anyone's laziness.

Sudha, however, suggested that mami should rest for a couple of hours before plunging into her daily chores and subsequent preparation for the trip. But when she returned to check up on mami, in the evening, she saw that her bags were already packed and she was lying down on a *mudha,* looking quite unwell. Mama had been pacing up and down the room looking extremely annoyed and worried. It seemed mami had been running a slight temperature since the day before and fearing that it would be an inconvenience to everyone, she had neither disclosed it nor taken any medication. Sudha could see that mama was simmering inside but restraining himself from speaking out.

Mami protested that too much was being made out of a slight temperature and there was no way she'd miss out on her Preeti's reception and that wonderful vacation in the resort. She retorted, "The only person, who ever told me that I too needed to relax, has been my son. He has been the only one who has offered me a vacation fit for a queen. And if you all think I am going to disappoint him now and miss out on this chance, because of a slight temperature, then you are really mistaken."

Mama put up his hands and said. "Fine, then do as you would. But I am not going to stand silently and watch you fool around with your health. If you still insist on going, then please go alone. I refuse to be a party to it."

This led to mami complaining and sulking, Sudha placating her and mama walking out of the house in a huff. The matter had turned complicated with each aggrieved party having its own justifiable point of view and each refusing to retreat. Another complication, hitherto unforeseen, had meanwhile cropped up. Minni who thought of herself as mami's official companion took an umbrage on being so left out.

The matter was ultimately settled with Madhukar's arbitration. It was decided that mami would take her medicine and complete rest for the next day, mama would graciously allow mami to go happily. Minni would accompany mami for the reception and the vacation but this would be the last time she would be allowed to bunk school for fun. So it all eventually ended well.

Finally Wednesday the 7th arrived. Mami was up and ready before the sunrise, full of excitement like a bird chirping away on the onset of spring. Mama true to his word was helpful and kind, persuading mami to take some extra money with her just in case. Minni jumped around in her bright yellow dress with leggings and full sleeves all excited to be going to a hill station with her best friend.

Sudha had made piping hot *matar poha* and *halwah* for breakfast and had packed some sandwiches for their journey, although she knew that Naresh would treat them all to elaborate meals all the way to Nainital.

Since the clock had struck nine and there was still no sign of the car, Madhukar offered to call up Naresh to find out if there had been a problem with the transport. Mami however had a different idea. She felt that there are always so many things cropping up in a house where such large scale events are organised. She said, "My poor son must be already so stressed out trying to get everyone ready and moving in time. There must be so many vehicles to look into, their drivers, provisions for the way, all the guests, their individual luggage, the luggage of the bride and presents for the groom's family. Just imagine missing out on any one of the above things and finding it out too late. I, as a mother, would not dream of bothering him any further. Madhukar if you do not mind, can you please drop us to Naresh's house. At least that'll be one load less on his mind."

No one could ever argue with a mother's heart and for once even mama thought that it was a sensible idea. So off the three of them left for Naresh's house. Mami was a little nervous as the scheduled time for departure was 9.30 a.m. in the morning, and it was already 9.20 a.m. by the time they were half way to his house.

It was such a relief to see the scene on Naresh's drive. There were around four cars and two SUVs all getting packed and ready to leave. The boots were being shut, final calls being made out to the couple of members locking up the house. Mami jumped out and ran dragging Minni along towards Naresh, with a victorious smile as if to say, "See I spared you the extra effort."

But what happened took everyone's breath away. Naresh looked at her incredulously and said, "Ija, what are you doing here? I don't think I asked you to come. Day before yesterday when I told the others to be ready, I didn't talk to you, did I? I'm sorry, but you are too old for such an outing and I really can't allow you to fall ill on me.

Ija, really sometimes you behave so foolishly and childishly. You really must show more dignity and restraint. Please go back. I'll try and see you when I come back, although with my new project, I don't think I'll have much time on hand."

Anandi mami stood there frozen, the words pounding inside her head with a force that could shatter the universe, her face as white as a sheet, her voice lost, her breath suspended and for a moment it was as if the earth had stopped moving. She had no idea of Minni's hand clutching at her or Madhukar coming in from behind, putting his arm around her shoulders and moving her back into his car. It was as if her whole being had been carved out of stone, beyond sensation, beyond feelings, numbed, frosted over, deadened.

Little children are at times the most perceptive and sensitive beings on earth. Minni who had no inkling of what had happened out there, could feel mami's trauma very acutely. And so for someone who always chattered nonstop, she did not utter a word or a sound all the way back.

Mama and Sudha were stunned to see them back home but mami's ashen face had the unspoken written all over it. Mama who'd taken a step towards her, sat down grimly on his mudha again, a defeated and bereft shadow spreading all over his face. Although very soon his usual silence had cloaked his bottomless anguish giving him that customary stoic appearance again.

Sudha followed mami who went straight to her temple and flung herself on the floor, letting out a heart wrenching wail which ripped through Sudha's heart. Mami broke down weeping inconsolably and Sudha who had never seen her so broken, so devastated, ever before, for once did not feel like using any skill or tact to console her.

It was impossible to believe that this was the same mami who could work untiringly every second of the day for even unknown people without a single expectation; the same mami who could see through people's pretences yet oblige them all, smiling away through the experience; the same mami who had borne her sons' apathy all along with an equanimity and grace which was indeed rare; who had become so broken, shattered and crushed.

Sudha saw a collage of events flashing through her mind; mami making prasad at Vinod da's house: mami decorating the floor with aipun; the temple with diyas; mami disheveled with her faded cotton sari with marks of turmeric and *geru* being left out from the photo session; Vinod da's amnesia of the old couple after the puja; flashes of known-unknown relatives cropping up like mushrooms all the while; mami going without her leisure to help anyone who requested; mami stitching falls for Preeti's saris; mami roasting spices; collecting ghee; making savories for the wedding; mami giving away her priceless bangle for Preeti; mami working, sweating, cooking, singing; mami silently nursing her fever lest it inconveniences the wedding; mami being rebuked in front of all and sundry as being foolish, childish, impetuous by the very son she had given birth to.

Numbed herself, Sudha had no words to offer and it appeared to her that neither did the idols in mami's temple, who for once were equally paralysed and desolate. It is at moments like these, she felt, that the universe hangs its head in disgrace, and that even God is comatose from shame.

✦ ✦ ✦

5

Reasons of the Heart

It was a fine handmade paper with around ten words scribbled on it in great haste. And I was marveling at how just ten words are enough to sweep the ground from under your feet.

"Devi left for her heavenly abode last night. Cremation tomorrow."

I kept staring incredulously at that distasteful intrusion in my life.

In my three decades of eventful and interesting life, death somehow had been the only alien factor. And now as I sat facing it, I felt none of the emotions I'd ever read or heard or seen in books, movies and life around me. All I felt was a sense of having been cheated and an inexplicable fury at this deception.

Devi knew that I was planning to visit her during the Puja holidays in October. I so wanted to talk to her about Ruma, the girl I wanted to spend my life with, about the marriage we were planning for December. There was so much I needed to talk and ask and share with her.

How could she walk away from me, just like that? How could she leave me so alone, so friendless in the middle of the night?

That was so unfair!

Whenever I think of Devi; I think of the strange paradigm of life and relationships.

Those relationships that life lines up for us, those that we hold gingerly and precariously, those that we work the most on are often the ones that leave us unmoved, untouched. As lifeless as the flowers we hold for puja in our sticky palm, neither alluring us with their beauty or fragrance nor tempting us to clasp them a moment longer; they are simply a ritual – hollow and meaningless.

Then there are the relationships that our hearts seek and find!

Relationships with the souls who feel like our lost mates, fragmented pieces of our unified whole; the souls that fill the deep abyss inside us spontaneously and absolutely and we have no reason, no logic to pick them out; except for a strange certainty that tells us, "Yes, this is it!" I understood it so clearly when I first met Devi.

I was a young Marketing Executive in a leading Tyre Company. Confident, ambitious and raring to go, I had accepted a new assignment in Ahmedabad, a completely new city for me after Delhi, where I had started my career two years ago. The only link I had there was a Mr. Sushant Pathak who worked in a bank and had come to Delhi soon after his marriage, fresh and eager to start his married life. My father then was looking around for a good, homely couple to rent out an independent portion of his bungalow.

Sushant Pathak was just what he had imagined an ideal tenant to be. And thus began a beautiful relationship between the two families. My mother welcomed Veena, his shy new bride with open arms, lovingly teaching her the essentials of homemaking.

In time they went back to Ahmedabad with a lovely daughter and a heart full of memories. Now that it was my turn to start a new life, my thoughts rushed to them and I immediately called them up. Just as I'd imagined, they were delighted to hear about my new assignment and a chance of our reuniting once again. Looking at their excitement any one could have mistaken me to be their long lost cousin. In Ahmedabad Veena met me exactly like she would her own younger brother. Both she and Mr. Pathak asked me to consider their home as mine and move in right away, but I was very clear about having an independent lodging preferably as a paying guest, which would also take care of my meals, laundry and other household chores.

It was precisely then that Veena remarked, "In that case why don't you stay with Devi?"

"Devi? Devi who?" I quipped. To which Sushant ji laughed and said, "Oh! Devi is Veena's mother, my mother-in-law."

I was totally aghast. "Well! Of all the things! You never call your mother by her name. What a family indeed. And what a mother to have allowed this form of address?" But the idea appealed to me. So off we all went to meet her.

Devi was nowhere near what I had imagined a 76 years old lonely widow to be. Of robust built and ample proportions, she had a booming voice which could put a church bell to shame. With eyes glowing with life and blazing with a fiery authority she could manage to have someone like me cowering in a corner.

She seemed to weigh me from all angles, asking me questions which, though apparently inane, were incisive and thorough. Finally she did approve, but by that time I wasn't sure if accepting this offer would be such a great idea after all.

Still with no other option in hand and with all the love that Veena and Sushant ji were showering me with, I found myself at her doorstep lock, stock and barrel, one fine day.

Living with Devi proved more difficult than I had ever thought it could be. She had her own set of rules laid out nice and proper. 8 p.m. was the dead line to be home every night, dinner at 9 p.m. No smoking, no drinking and no phone calls after 9 p.m. There were no mobiles back then. Partying to be limited to once a month and even then one had to be back by 11 p.m. after which the gate would be locked for the night. I would be required to pay the charges for my upkeep on the third of every month failing which there would an extra penalty of twenty rupees for every day of the delay.

I would have upped and left but for the fact that my office was a stone's throw from her house, and I actually didn't smoke, drink or even party as such. Instead after a hard day's work I craved to be with my books, music and my solitude. But the resentment at being restricted so, stayed strong within.

Over the days unknowingly, unhampered by the initial resentment, Devi and I fell into a comfortable rhythm. In our silences we forged a strange communication. There was an underlying respect and silent appreciation for each other.

Although if someone had asked us, I was sure, we both would've vehemently denied it in the first instant.

Then slowly, tentatively we started probing each other's space, just like two puppies do, smelling each other gingerly, apprehensively, wishfully, wanting to strike a new friendship.

For instance, one fine day, Devi came and announced indifferently, that if I wished, I could join her in the living room to watch the Television, or that I may pick up the magazines from the living room, provided I returned them after reading, both the offers being bliss for me.

Similarly, I too found myself asking her if she wanted me to run some errands for her since I was going to the market anyways. Or if I could water her plants on Sundays as I used her hose pipe to wash my motorcycle. I kept telling myself that it was really nothing because I had always loved gardening and she did have a nice garden after all.

Over the time I found that Devi would cook more and more of the dishes I seemed to relish. A couple of times I found that a broken button on my shirt was sewed back, a tear mended, the socks darned without so much as a mention from her.

And then one day I met with a major accident. My motor cycle was thrown off balance by a speeding jeep, driven by a gang of boys high on liquor. Passers-by brought me home but there was a deep concussion, amnesia and loss of blood. I don't know how she managed it, but she did get me instant medical help and was constantly by my side like a cow with her calf. In between the waves of my consciousness, I could see her keeping nonstop vigil by my bed side, putting ice cold strips on my forehead, feeding me spoons full of broth and also taking my temperature at short intervals.

In life very often, 'all that' our caution and inhibitions do not allow us to express, flows out unheeded, unrestrained, unabashedly the very moment 'fear of losing' dawns on us.

My vulnerability along with her anxiety broke down every wall of reserve and diffidence between us. The need of pretense was over and as I healed and grew stronger, we found ourselves bonding with an ease and spontaneity that was both refreshing and exhilarating.

We were friends, confidantes, mother and son.

I could talk to her like I could with none other, not even my family. She was a wonderful listener. She never judged, never sermonised, never moralised. She simply gave a concerned and fond hearing every time I felt like unwinding or releasing my pent up feelings.

She seemed to have found a surrogate son, a man Friday and a loving companion in me. My presence had wiped away her loneliness and all the silences that had clustered round her in that empty house. She probably had her own demons to ward off and maybe in some inexplicable way I was bringing alleviation.

Her husband had been a professor of English, a very erudite, scholarly man. He wanted to marry an equally educated girl, but in those days, in India, marriages were arranged by the heads of the families, invariably grandparents and most of the times even the parents had no say in the final selection. Devi was unfortunately neither formally educated nor a conventionally beautiful girl. All her goodness and efforts somehow could not bridge the emotional chasm between the man of her dreams and her.

His frustration and his revolt against the entire system, against the injustice wrought on him burst out vide his revulsion and apathy against that young defenseless soul.

Devi accepted it as her lot with the patience and tolerance of a woman who has the maturity to understand, accept and yet care. However, when this apathy was passed on like a baton to the heir apparent, she was shattered.

But the die was cast.

When her son Nanu left for Connecticut to pursue his studies, she felt an eerie chill, a sinister fear creeping into her; seeping right down to her bones. She somehow knew that this was the end of the road for both of them as fellow travellers. This grown up young man who she had cradled in her womb for nine months, was now a stranger, with only a face that looked familiar and nothing else.

She was so right. Nanu completed his Computer Engineering and took up a job right there, in due course. At first there were phone calls every second day, then every week, then once a month and slowly they petered down to an occasional call on New Year and birthdays. In time he found an American girl, married her and applied for the required Green Card like any other good Indian boy.

Devi never spoke about this emotional defection to Veena who like a traditional Indian girl had got too busy with her new family, in-laws, husband and having babies. She was a sweet, loving daughter but as all relationships go, her mother too was a means to an end, a facilitator for her life; never a woman, a person, a soul who had feelings, emotions and could hurt too.

If Veena and Nanu could know how wounded Devi felt inside her carefree, happy demeanor they'd definitely have been embarrassed. According to them mothers were just not supposed to feel. They were not supposed to be human beings with desires, longings, cravings, with hurts, wounds, anguish and emotional scars.

But I could reach out to the person, the woman, the child in her, and could very vividly read her wounds and gashes without her having to say a word to me. For me her beauty lay not in her strength to bear the sufferings, but in the spirit with which she did so. Not simply in the tenacity of her love, but also in the fragility of her emotions.

Her liveliness, her gutsiness, her indefatigable joie de vivre were simply exemplary. She taught me that you are not defeated till you actually surrender.

We learnt to laugh off the disappointments and hang on to hope, we learnt to blow away the dark clouds and keep the silver lining as bonus, we learnt to transform every sob into a song. We talked endlessly till late night, swaying on the *jhoola* a bench like swing, listening to old melodies. We cooked together, went out shopping, watched an occasional movie and sometimes indulged in *gol gappas* and *chaat* shamelessly on the road side. We were so well bonded, so in tune with each other that we could have put the closest pair of mother and son to shame, for sure.

But good things rarely last long. One day too soon, I was informed of my promotion and transfer back to Delhi. Completely taken aback, I requested them to let me stay. My boss actually looked at me like I had lost my senses. My pleas fell on deaf ears.

Devi once again surprised me by her stoic acceptance of this move. Sometimes I feel it was truly that reaction of hers, which gave me the strength to carry on. She helped me pack and pooh-poohed at my dejection. Who knows if it was her way to ward off the melancholy and tears?

On the last day as I sat down in the cab, the final good byes stuck somewhere in that lump in my throat, the unexpressed anguish glistening on my lashes, she pushed a cloth bag into my hands and said, "Sonny, this is yours. Take it."

As I pulled the drawstrings, I saw wads of notes peeping out. It was all the money that I had given to her on the third of every month, along with the occasional penalties for defaults. I could recognise a couple of signed notes too.

I just couldn't believe it. So she had demanded all that currency, for nothing. She actually didn't spend any money on herself or the house. But why?

She smiled at my bewilderment and replied, "I'm a mother after all. I know how you children love to splurge all your money without any thought of tomorrow. I had connected with you the moment I saw you sonny. I knew you were a wonderful boy. So I decided to ask you for a rent, which I had planned to keep away, as your saving every month. Now since this is rightfully my money, I want you to invest it wisely. When you finally get married, I want you to buy something important for your home with this money." She then winked and said, "And mind you, I also want to see the girl before you tie the knot."

Tears were flowing away unabashedly by now and I really couldn't care, what anyone thought about me anymore. I waved her a good bye, little knowing that this was the last I'd be seeing of her.

As the letter fluttered in my hand, I could see the smudged words paying tribute to that lovely soul, who was truly no one to me and yet was, all in all!

My tears were flowing wantonly now, every drop paying a homage to that beautiful soul,

"I love you Devi. Be happy wherever you are."

✦ ✦ ✦

6

Justice for Janaki

Monday:

Silence has a language of its own. So often silences convey much more than could ever be expressed through words or sound.

Uma had never felt this more strongly than as she felt on the day, which now she wished had never dawned on her. That morning had been like any other Monday morning, somber and ordinary. But as she approached the staff room of her all girls' college, she could feel the ghastly silence whispering to her ominously. She had this eerie desire to simply turn away and leave but then the very next minute she found her own foolishness so embarrassing.

As she entered the room her glance fell on Aditi and their group sitting in a corner, a look of extreme consternation on their faces. A feeling of alarm flashed through her. Uma knew without being told that something untoward had occurred for sure. She saw Aditi beckoning her to come and join them. With great trepidation she complied noticing from the corner of her eyes the group of senior professors at the other end of the long table huddled together.

As she sat down Aditi whispered "Janaki is no more. She died today morning, beaten to death by her husband." Uma looked at her bewildered, not understanding a word of what Aditi had said. The news simply refused to make sense. 'Janaki is no more' was about as implausible as someone telling her that the birds had stopped chirping or that the sun would not shine anymore. The very thought of Janaki brought to her mind the liveliest face she had ever seen, eyes dancing in merriment, lips donning the most infectious smile, tinkling laughter like a freely falling cascade in the wilderness and colors bright, vibrant, vivacious. How could so much life be 'no more'?

She barely managed to whisper, "Janaki? Oh no, It is impossible."

Aditi squeezed her hand understandingly and said, "I know Uma, its hard to believe, but its true. The principal had got a call early morning from the police asking her to come and identify the body at the Government Hospital. She just came back and told us all. It was Janaki, beaten to death by that good-for-nothing drunkard husband of hers. Could you believe it, the entire night he beat her brutally, mercilessly till she could hold on to her life no more."

Uma shuddered involuntarily. The very thought of such bestiality, such helplessness and such a violent end sent shivers down her spine. A strange sense of melancholy and shame washed over her but before she could be drowned in its vastness, Madhavi Prakash, their professor of psychology, a diehard feminist, announced that cars had been organised for those who wanted to go and pay their last respects to the departed soul.

All of them moved out. Uma, who was beyond any thought, feeling or action, felt herself being pushed by Aditi into the last awaiting vehicle. The car was jam packed with everyone talking at the same time, everyone suddenly aroused from their ennui and competing to express grief at such a gruesome death.

The strangest thing about tragedies is that as long as they are not in our orbit, they are interesting, a source of great conversation and opportunity to share our wisdom. Tragedies that befall others often leave us with a convoluted sense of relief. Such misfortunes, often unknown to ourselves, offer us sadistic consolation and comfort.

Incidentally, for Uma it was a tragedy that left her deeply bereft. Lost to everyone else she had quietly withdrawn into her own world and looking out of the speeding car, she watched the past roll by along with the sliding landscape.

It had all started ten years back when Dr. Shiv Bharadwaj, her husband, had joined a leading multi specialty hospital in Jaipur as a specialist in Neurosurgery. It was a big move for them from Lucknow and this move threatened to derail Uma's otherwise flourishing career, that of teaching B.A. English Honours in the prestigious IT College of Lucknow. However, owing to a sudden coincidental vacancy and her IT college reference, she got an immediate lectureship in one of the renowned girls' college of Jaipur.

She could still recall so vividly how extremely anxious she had been as she had walked into the staff room, on her first day in the college. As a reserved and reticent person, despite the nature of her job which demanded excellent communication skills and smooth interaction, she had somehow always found it difficult, to open out to strangers and make friends easily. Her nervousness was therefore quite apparent and palpable, as she sat down in far corner of the room and vainly dabbed the droplets of cold perspiration that had appeared on her forehead. She could feel her hands turning cold and moist, her lips turning dry and her throat parched from the acute anxiety that being in a strange place, among new people invariably brings.

As she was struggling to hang on to her composure albeit vainly, Janaki came into her life for the first time, in form of a pair of graceful hands offering her a glass of chilled water. The first look often sows the seed of many lifelong relationships. Often it ignites dormant memories of past births buried deep in the subconscious and unknown soul connections over many lives. They flash into our consciousness with a certainty that no reason or logic dare ever negate.

Grateful for that glass of water, Uma had looked up to see a pair of smiling eyes looking at her with such compassion and understanding that she felt strangely comforted. The look was followed by a soft voice that said, "Its always like this on the first day with everyone, didi. You'll be fine tomorrow. If you need assistance, I'm around." And then as an afterthought she smiled and said, "Didi, I'm Janaki, ayah of this staff room." Uma looked at her again, this time a complete, more lingering look and saw to her surprise a slender, petite woman with a refreshingly pretty face and the largest pair of eyes she had ever seen. Her hair drawn back into a thick plait hung much below her waist. Long time after when Uma had teased her saying that if she could've had hair as long and thick as hers, she would have used them as a cushion to sit down on, Janaki had looked at her piteously and said, "Didi they say that long hair like mine only bring misfortune and marital unhappiness. Pray to God that you are never cursed with such hair."

Maybe it was something to do with that first connect or maybe it was just coincidental but as the time passed, their association grew from amiable small talk to much more meaningful conversations and a mutual respect for each other. Uma noticed how Janaki stood apart from the other class four employees in her demeanour, in her soft cultured voice and her professional conduct. Janaki too for reasons of her own felt drawn towards the new lecturer of English from Lucknow.

Initially it was Janaki who alerted Uma regarding the bullies of the third year, the pranksters and the spoilt ones. She would quietly come and forewarn her about the group that was planning to bunk the class that day and where exactly could she find them in the campus. She would remind her regularly about the departmental meetings and made sure that Uma reached there on time. There were times when her senior colleagues would change the time or the venue of a certain meeting at the last minute without proper intimation but Janaki would rush to tip her off the minute she got the wind of it. As a result Uma could attend each and every meeting, no matter when, no matter where. Her sincerity and consistency won her a grudging respect from the departmental head and seniors.

Around six months after Uma had joined the college, it was announced that special tutorials shall be held for the weaker students. Since most of the students were extremely weak in English owing to the comparatively poor standard of the Rajasthan State Higher Secondary Board, Uma was required to stay back every alternate day for additional three hours after the college time. The tutorials started after an hour of the regular closing time, which was the time given to the students to refresh themselves and catch a quick bite in the college canteen. It was at times like these that Janaki would fetch her a cup of tea from the staff pantry or would hover around her in the staff room. At times they would strike a conversation and it was during such moments that Janaki would exclaim, "Didi, I feel that people are poor not because they lack wealth but they are poor because they lack education. I really wanted to study but my parents were scared that the more I studied, more difficult it would be for them to get me a match."

Sometimes she would ask sharply, "Didi, why is being born a girl such a curse? And why is getting her married off the only concern of parents? Is marriage all that she has in her life? What about life itself? Is that really of no consequence at all? You are wise, tell me is it actually poverty which makes people so dogmatic or is it the lack of knowledge?"

Uma had never found herself as speechless in front of any audience as she often did in front of this tenth standard passed woman with her simple queries. But what could anyone really say to someone who had all along been a bright, enthusiastic student and was still denied her basic right to study? What could one say to a woman who was full of life, joy and hope but was married off at sixteen to a labourer on daily wages whose evenings were drowned in cheap liquor; to a woman who had been physically and verbally harassed by her near blind mother-in-law from the very first day? What could one say to someone who had her first child at seventeen, followed by two forced abortions and finally a son when she turned twenty two?

Janaki would often talk about her childhood days in Bikaner, the happy, fun filled, carefree days of school and books, of fooling around with friends, playing in the vast open spaces on the sand, eating *ber*, *amla* and imli on the sly under the huge *peepal* trees and weaving dreams of becoming a teacher one day, standing in front of a blackboard with around thirty students looking at her in awe – ah, the sheer joy and pride of it. Janaki's eyes twinkled in a million hues as she reminisced about those gone by days. She would talk about her two younger sisters Parvati and Meera and how all three of them played *gitte, sitolia, stepu, aankh micholi* and would spend hours making sand castles. She would talk about her mother and the fresh hot rotis she'd cook for them on the *chulha*, about that red garlic chutney the flavour of which was still so fresh on her tongue. She would remember the Dal-baati-choorma they all had sitting near the slow simmering angithi and how her mother cooked each baati to perfection, baking it just so, inside the hot ashes at the bottom of the angithi.

Janaki would often sigh and say, "Didi, happy childhood is an opium by itself. It gives you a euphoria that is indescribable and creates fantasies of its own. Your imagination soars high and no dream appears unattainable."

She would continue, "I cannot blame my parents for what they did. They were simple people with insecurities and compulsions. I'm just upset with the whole system which forbids a girl child her right to a complete life and at times even existence. Didi, I want my daughter 'Vatsala' to live as a human being in her own right. I want her to live not simply as a woman, an extension to someone else, a slave, but to live limitlessly, spreading her wings out soaring high."

Janaki was truly keen to turn this dream into a reality. It was as if she was driven with a fire, a frenzy, an obsession to make this possible. It was as if this one burning ambition gave her the reason to live, a reason to fight on despite all odds in her life.

Uma agreed to help her secure an admission for Vatsala in a prestigious missionary school under their special quota for underprivileged children. At home, Shiv thought that the whole idea was quite foolish and Uma was being far too impulsive for her own good. Opposition notwithstanding, Uma took up the project single handedly and managed the feat. Janaki was beyond herself with joy and bending down to touch her feet she exclaimed, "You must have been my mother in some birth. Only a mother could have done so much, so selflessly. Didi bless me so that all my dreams for my daughter may come true. Pray that she be as well read, as courageous as you and that she may mould many more young minds with knowledge and grace."

Janaki's reactions and responses would often leave Uma speechless. There was something about her character, her fabric which seemed so incongruent with her socio-economic background. The coarseness, the dissatisfaction, the greed so common in her other counterparts, was missing in her entirely. She had an unwavering belief in the fairness of life and goodness. Despite all adversities she had managed to retain her intrinsic faith, dreams and that basic sweetness which refused to turn bitter or cynical. Her thoughts were amazingly refined and profound.

Over the next couple of years Uma could feel the bond between them, growing deeper and stronger. Slowly over the time Janaki had taken to confiding in Uma far more easily and frequently, which was an indication of her growing trust and faith in her. The more Uma learnt about her, the more she realised that pain and sufferings are such universal emotions. Women all over the world across education and class lines struggle for their identities, in just about the same way. Similarly, in just about the same way sense of power brings out the animal in man.

Janaki however looked at it differently. She would often counter, "Violence is the expression of a frightened soul didi. Every act of brutality hides a million fears, a million insecurities. Anger is truly the ultimate sign of helplessness."

Uma would be astounded by such a statement, coming from a woman who would be walking every other day into the staff room, covering her waist, her back or her forehead, trying pathetically to hide the black blue weals of the last night's violence. So many times after being sworn by Uma, under the name of every possible emotion, would she acknowledge the tortures meted out to her? Finally, one day Uma lost her hitherto maintained composure and cried out exasperatedly, "Just how can you accept such a bestial behaviour from a man who's a wastrel through and through? You are his wife Janaki, not his slave. How dare he be so brutal with you? You, who are running the whole house, doing all the domestic chores, looking after his mother, children and him? This is really so inhuman and unfair."

"So are so many other things in life didi." Janaki said wistfully with a dismal smile, "Tell me, what is not unfair? I am really not the only martyr around. Every night women are abused and brutalised in our *jhuggis*. Pain and tears are a woman's lot, didi. Marriages are made in heaven. Who are we to question God's decision for us? In our religion a husband is a woman's ultimate God. We are brought up with the belief that a girl is her husband's, and thereby also her in-laws' property, to be handed over to them at the time of marriage. Parents are merely custodians of their daughters, nothing more.

"Didi, my husband Narain's father was a very poor farmer of Sinthal village in Bikaner. Narain was born weak and succumbed to polio which paralysed his right leg forever. As a boy he wasn't very fond of studies; however he was extremely fascinated by the master potter of his village and would often bunk school to watch him rotate the wheel. Over time observing the potter keenly, he picked up the finer intricacies of the technique including the kneading, pinching, moulding, glazing of the clay and firing the pots to perfection. On seeing his aptitude and enthusiasm the potter took him on as an apprentice and in no time Narain had mastered the craft. He even started introducing new items and ideas to woo the customers, especially children.

"It was then that the great famine of 1979 gripped the whole of Bikaner and its neighbouring villages. There was a mass exodus from my husband's village and all the farmers and artisans migrated to bigger cities like Jodhpur, Jaipur, Kota and Ajmer. Narain came to Jaipur, but here the existing potters were already facing a tough time due to the flux in market requirements. Clay pots were no longer in demand. So he was compelled to work as a labourer on daily wages in a construction site. It was arduous work, and my husband was not really made for it. His artistic soul felt tortured and stifled. But he had to feed his mother and himself, so there was no choice for him.

"Now tell me didi, was that not unfair? In the meantime, I was married off to him. He was not ready for marriage but his mother who had lost her eyes to Glaucoma insisted that she couldn't carry on with the household chores anymore and she herself needed to be looked after and served at this stage of life. Since he was the only surviving son, it was his moral duty to marry for her sake. He liked me but I too was a burden and liability for him. One more mouth to feed, where there was no money.

"Incidentally, his work life too was getting tougher and more complicated. He had neither the stamina nor the will for such grueling physical labour and would often lose his temper on his co workers and supervisor. As a result they avoided him and there were many days when he was not called for work.

"He then took all my jewellery and bought a secondhand potter-wheel from an erstwhile potter who had closed shop, finding it extremely difficult to survive in the market. For a few days, he was very happy and excited about this new venture and this was the time when Vatsala came into our life. However, slowly he found that there were no takers for mud items in the fast changing city. Even the mud toys that were so loved in Sinthal went unappreciated by the children here. This further crushed all his confidence in himself and filled him up with bitterness and anger against the situations and his destiny.

So tell me didi, was that not unfair?

"With no job and no hope of any work, he ended up mixing with bad company and started wiling away his time in cards and alcohol. In the meantime, I'd conceived twice, but both the times, my mother-in-law took me to a sleazy clinic, where finding out that I had conceived daughters on both times; she got them to murder my babies in the womb itself. As per my upbringing, it is sacrilege to talk back to your mother-in-law and I simply could not utter a word. She further filled up my husband's ears by saying that I was the cursed one who'd never be able to bear him a son. This further antagonised him and he started shouting and hitting out at me. Very soon violence became his release for all the pent up rage and fury within him. I could've protested, but the irony was, I knew where the anger was coming from. It was his fear of the future, the dark looming clouds of uncertainty that was killing everything beautiful and joyous in him.

"Need for survival gnaws into our character, eating into it slowly, corroding it, just like weevils infesting the grains slowly, silently and ruining them forever. My husband was not cruel by nature, but the pressures of survival were far too heavy on his shoulders and he was crushed under it. I do wish at times that he could have been stronger and more resilient. But you can't condemn a person for his weakness, can you?

"During this time, I had started doing part time jobs as a house maid in the nearby houses. I came across some very kind ladies. One of them who was a professor in this college was very happy with my zeal and sincerity. They needed a couple of ayahs in the college and she recommended me strongly. My having passed the tenth class did the rest. This came as a huge economic help to my family in our days of starvation.

Although it provided additional reasons for Narain to pick up more fights with me every day. At times I wished he had got some education; things would have been very different then. Knowledge makes you more tolerant to adversities and more adaptable to changes. Narain was deprived of all these mercies because he refused to open his mind to information, learning and awareness.

"In about a year I was made permanent and the next year I had my son Amit with full facility of maternity leaves.

"All this while, my mother-in-law did her best to pile me up with all the household chores. Her speech as everyone knows is acerbic and no matter how much I worked, she still had reasons to scald me with her vitriolic words. It hurt me, made me cry.

"But didi, I know that she's had the most miserable life herself and unlike me she has no hopes to live for, no dreams to accomplish. My father-in-law died when Narain was five years old and she was forced to work her bones off as a farm laborer in the scorching heat of summers, the freezing cold of winters, in pouring rain, in health and in sickness, in exchange of a paltry sum of money. All those years, there was no one she could count on for support or comfort. Being a widow, she was considered inauspicious and a social pariah. Her in-laws insulted her constantly with barbs about her evil shadow on their son. She was ostracised socially and humiliated at every instant. More than the poverty, it was this social isolation that crushed her and made her resent her fate. To add on to her miseries her Glaucoma, the silent killer of vision, had already turned her near blind. Although she fought on bravely, but the pent-up hurt, resentment and unshared anguish deep inside, killed all that was sweet and feminine in her. The world taught her that there is no sensitivity, no compassion, and no mercy for the unfortunate and the weak. Now tell me didi, was that not unfair?"

Having spoken in one frenzied breath, face flushed with her own emotions, Janaki paused to get a grip on herself once again. Uma gazed at her speechlessly, marveling at how amazing that simple woman was. For all the unfairness that life had piled on to her, for all the excesses that she bore physically and for all the humiliation that she suffered everyday in front of her own children and mother-in-law; there was none of the bitterness, cynicism or rancour that was normal. She was so unlike the mute sufferers of her class, who submitted unquestioningly to violence, because there was no option. On the contrary, she did feel the indignity very strongly but was generous enough to see beyond herself, into the fears and complexes of her oppressors. Her silences were born not out of her helplessness but more out of her larger sense of empathy and compassion.

The more Uma understood her, the more she respected her tolerance and resilience. Although at times she would still try to provoke her in mock anger by saying, "Next time you too pick up a stick and beat him back Janaki, will you?" And Janaki would giggle at the ridiculous image this thought would conjure up for her.

Realising that there wasn't much she could do vis-à-vis Janaki's domestic harassment, Uma encouraged her to have a firmer grip on her finances. This would enable her to do all that was necessary for her children, provide for their higher studies in due course and give her that self assurance which she desperately needed as a battered woman. She got Janaki to open her account in a leading bank whose branch was adjacent to their college building. When the government upgraded their scales under the pay commission, Uma bulldozed her into putting all her arrears in a fixed deposit in the name of Vatsala. Janaki was initially horrified and exclaimed, "Didi, that would be cheating my husband and breaking my marriage vows, wouldn't it? And what if he ever learnt about it? I'm sure he'd kill me." But Uma overruled all her objections and fears, "Marriage vows weren't for you alone Janaki. As per our Hindu marriage, the husband also vows to provide for, love and protect his wife from all adversities in life. Narain has done just the opposite of that, but no one questions him. You're saving the money for fulfilling his side of the vows too, to provide for his children, mother and him in sickness and hunger. Janaki this money is totally unexpected and you don't have to account for it. If you tell your husband about it, he'll drink it away too. Think about your children's future and happiness Janaki."

Finally Janaki had relented and the fairly hefty amount of arrears was siphoned off smoothly into Vatsala's name with Uma as the nominated guardian. Janaki was very insistent about the latter. "Didi," she'd said, "I feel my money would be much safer under your eye. You can reinvest it again for my Vatsala, till the time she really needs it. And with you around, there's no chance of Narain getting to know about it or coercing you into giving this money to him."

From then on the additional money was safely deposited every month in Janaki's account in the bank. Over the years it accumulated into a good sum of money which made her thank Uma so profusely over and over again that Uma would scream in mock anger, "Janaki, one more word and I'll resign from being the nominee in all your accounts." This would subdue Janaki's surge of emotion, much to Uma's relief...

Time sailed by. Uma got promoted from a lecturer to the position of Assistant professor over a spate of back breaking refresher courses, assessments and interviews. Janaki too got upgraded from lower salary grade to the higher one. Vatsala had picked up her mother's passion and hunger for studies and was doing extremely well in her ninth standard.

Once when Janaki was suffering from a bad bout of typhoid and had been on leave for over a week, Uma had taken her address from the administration department and had gone over to meet her with some fruits, sweets and gifts for her children. Walking through the filthy alleys of that slum settlement, amidst general squalor, impoverished, dark and dingy shanties, people crowding around a solitary municipal tap, clogged drains, garbage heaps, faeces lying on the sides, flies and stink; her heart sank to think of how unfair is life to some. Life which should have embraced each of its children with equal ardour, treats an entire lot with contempt and derision. No wonder these alleys nurture antagonism, crime, hostility and simmering aggression deep within.

However, walking into Janaki's home was like entering a different world within that macrocosm of grime, filthiness and destitution. Suddenly it was so evident to her, why Janaki had always stood out from the others. Her intrinsic grace was so evident in the cleanliness, orderliness and simplicity of her abode. A small *Tulsi ka chaura* greeted her just outside the door, a faded, clean cotton sari, cleverly improvised as a curtain swayed gently at the door. Inside the only room which housed five people was spotlessly clean with a wooden cot at one end and a small kitchen at the other. A quick sneaking glance revealed sparkling albeit mismatched crockery and utensils arranged neatly on a much used stand, text books (possibly Vatsala's) stacked in wooden shelves nailed on a wall, a small black and white TV and a money plant cutting in an empty milk bottle standing boldly at the window sill in all its glory. Janaki lying on a thick mattress on the floor was surprised, embarrassed, delighted all at the same time. She introduced Uma to her mother-in-law, a shriveled, old, pathetic woman with gnarled fingers and a pronounced stoop that somehow spoke of the back breaking burdens which life had piled up on her so unfairly. As Uma recalled all the horrific acts of this wretched septuagenarian, she felt amazed at how life at times touches a simple, normal soul with misery and pain and turns him into the ugliest, vilest creature imaginable. It reminded her of the fairy tales wherein the evil witch curses an innocent prince and turns him into a monstrous, repugnant, dwarf.

While Uma was getting acquainted with Janaki's mother-in-law, Vatsala who had just come back from school, peeped in from behind the door. Their eyes met, the younger one's curious and diffident and the elder one's brimming with mirth and warmth. Uma beckoned her with a gentle look and she came in shyly, yet willingly. Tall, willowy, graceful, charming, a spitting image of her mother, she was every bit as spontaneous, lively and joyous as her. And just like Janaki would've been, she was far more delighted with her new books than the sweets that Uma had got for her. She was everything Uma would have loved to have in a daughter of her own, especially her sharp mind and a love for books apart from a keen sensitivity which incidentally made Janaki extremely anxious and worried about her. Janaki's son Amit was, as all ten year old boys are, far too involved in his game of marbles, to respond to the new visitor but was quite happy with the unexpected gift of chocolates from her.

This visit though small and perfunctory gave Uma a still clearer insight into Janaki's tough life and the stressful battles she was fighting all along.

Uma's train of thoughts was broken as the car suddenly screeched to a halt. They had arrived outside the slum settlement and the cars could go no further. Most of the faculty was already there. Madhavi Prakash had taken the initiative and appointed herself as the leader of the whole team. As they approached the group, Uma could hear her saying, "Let's all make a single file and walk up to her house. I request all of you to hold peace in respect of the departed soul and not to react even if you see her husband around. We will voice our protest and fury against that fiend's barbaric act after her cremation is over and I give you my word that we will definitely have him punished for her murder very soon."

Madhavi had a way of saying the most appealing things at the right time and so everyone followed her instructions without a murmur. Although Uma could hear a couple of her colleagues mumbling that if they were to see her husband around, they wouldn't be responsible for their action. Nearly all of them felt that he should also be beaten to death and hanged publically, to show everyone, that no longer can you brutalise women and get away with it.

However, the scene at Janaki's house was something no one was mentally prepared for. Right outside near her own Tulsi ka chaura lay the woman who had embraced life lovingly and joyously.

'She' – whose eyes danced merrily, whose laughter fell on ears like a thousand bangles jingling together, whose love for life was like a river gushing forwards in full stream – surging, rushing, swooshing and then meandering through the rocky and rough terrains to reach her destination, 'she' who desired nothing but a right to live with freedom and dignity, 'she' who had dreams for her children – dreams of flying free, soaring high and seeking newer horizons for themselves, all that was denied to her in her life, now laid broken, defeated and lifeless.

Uma looked at her beautiful face now black and deep purple, her eyes swollen, lips lacerated, blood dried up near the ears all bearing witness to the last night's barbarism and savagery. Her body was covered in a white sheet with a few marigold garlands carelessly thrown around her. The entire settlement seemed to have gathered there and the moment the college staff approached the body, there was a sudden onslaught of wailing and lamenting and some of the women got carried away into beating their chests and pulling their hair in an aggressive competition of grief. Uma spotted Vatsala hiding behind the door, a numb shock writ large in her eyes. She softly sneaked away from her group and inching behind the crowd made her way to the little lost girl whom she hugged tightly, too sad and dejected to offer any consolation. Janaki's mother-in-law sat wailing at a corner, babbling incoherently and cursing her son and daughter-in-law in the same breath. The young boy sitting near his grandmother was busy digging into a packet of chips, which probably some well meaning neighbour had handed him in sympathy and concern.

A few minutes later, a few neighbours came and took the mother-in-law out to have a last look at Janaki. The wailing rose to a crescendo. Uma noticed that Janaki had been given her last bath and was now decked up in a red shimmering sari, bright red sindoor stuffed all the way into the central parting of her hair, her *mangalsutra*, her red bangles, her *bichhuas*, her nath all kept on her chest, for she had died a *suhaagin* and was therefore the auspicious one. The marigold garlands now more profusely covering her from head to toe, hid her wounds admirably.

One look at Janaki, and the old woman fell down crying and pleading with her, to open her eyes and wake up, to have mercy on her little children, blind mother-in-law and her husband who had been detained by the police for investigation. Seeing no movement despite her pleas, watching her lifeless body lay still, she began cursing her for being far too fussy and delicate for her own situation. Screaming exasperatedly she ranted, "All the men in this jhuggi beat their wives every day, but the wives are still up and about the next day. Only this mem-saab here had to enact this drama on my poor son. Mark my words; she'll get up as soon as the funeral pyre starts burning. Just see if she doesn't."

Before the mood could get violent, the neighbours dragged the woman away and the procession started for the crematorium ground. Within minutes the place was cleared of the body, the crowd, the voices and the tears. A life had disappeared, sublimating into nothingness. All the beauty, the grace, joys, laughter, longings, desires, all the dreams vaporised into nihility. A candle blown off in a single whiff and a piercing darkness left behind for those who had once seen the light.

Once outside the slum, Madhavi Prakash had once again taken the podium and was thanking everyone for their sensitivity and for sparing the time and effort for a class four employee of the college. She said that since it had been an emotionally distressing day, she had requested the principal to allow them to go home straight from there and the permission had been granted. She further added, "Well, this is the most deplorable case of domestic violence, woman harassment and torture that we could ever across in this time and age. This is not only a breach of our constitution but is also a breach of the basic tenets of humanity and decency. As thinking citizens of this country, as human beings who believe in the dignity of life, and above all as women and therefore as sisters, I'm sure you all must be equally affronted and furious at the bestiality of that depraved man. As those whose mission it is to guide and mould the youth, specially women of tomorrow, to teach them to respect themselves and fight against all injustice; it becomes our moral duty to fight for Janaki and get her justice if only posthumously. So let's all meet tomorrow in the staff room during the lunch hour and work out the detailed strategy of this fight."

There was something about Madhavi that always fascinated Uma. She spoke with so much elan and intensity that the entire crowd was swept away in her speech and passion. Rarely could anyone fault her in her logic and conviction. And what was more, if required, she spoke with such emotional fervour that the audience would unfailingly be moved to tears.

Tuesday:

The Madhavi magic proved itself once again, in the enthusiastically full attendance at lunch hour in the staff room, the very next day. Madhavi herself was in deep discussion with five of the other senior professors of the faculty one of whom Uma identified as Rekha Srivastava of the Hindi department, a very powerful orator with an equally influential political clout and the other Ms Puja Bhasin, a confirmed spinster and a misandrist known for her feminist ideals. Then there was Anita Pratap who wrote a weekly column in the leading Hindi daily of Jaipur. Her husband Om Pratap was the Editor-in-chief of the same daily and had been an editor of a major National Hindi daily prior to this assignment. Anita was known for her effective media networking. Sitting alongside and making some notes was Mrs. Rachna Joshi, whose husband was a renowned criminal lawyer of the Rajasthan High Court – Jaipur bench and was known for his political aspirations. And finally there was Saroj Singh, professor of Political Science and wife of Gajendra Singh, MP of the leading opposition party. Saroj Singh had been actively campaigning for women's causes for the past decade and was known for relentless perusal of woman abuse offenders and getting grievance redressal.

As soon as all had collected, Madhavi stood up and thanked everyone for supporting the cause of injustice against women. She said, "My colleagues and friends, if Janaki's soul could be watching us right now then I'm sure it would find immense comfort in the knowledge that her fight was not wasted, that she did not die a lost and defeated woman, that we are fighting her case and shall not rest until we could have that murderer hanged by his neck till he dies.

"We have selected a team of five members namely Mrs. Rekha Srivastava, Ms. Puja Bhasin, Mrs. Anita Pratap, Mrs. Rachna Joshi and Mrs. Saroj Singh. They will follow up Janaki's case with the police, the Rajasthan State Women's Commission and finally the National Commission of Women. Mrs. Anita Pratap has promised us all media support at the state and national level, Mrs. Rachna Joshi has already requested Mr. Narendra Joshi, renowned criminal lawyer and her husband to take up this case on philanthropic grounds from the sessions court onwards as a very special favour without any remuneration. Mrs. Saroj Singh would be organising the campaign 'Justice for Janaki' all over the city. She would also rope in the opposition party and they've promised to raise this issue in the state legislative assembly if possible. While on the subject we have also decided to organise a 'Candle Light March' this Saturday from 6.30 p.m. to 8.30 p.m. from 'Collectorate Circle' to the 'Statue Circle' to raise our voices for quick justice to Janaki.

"So let us all gear up and give full cooperation to the campaign and the 'Candle Light March'. Kindly talk to your students about it and garner all support from them too. It is high time we as women stood up for each other and facilitated in erasing the blight of domestic violence altogether."

Madhavi's words were like magic potion and by the end of the speech everyone could feel adrenalin rushing through their veins. The room was charged up and you could actually feel the energy crackling in the air. The meeting ended, and they all dispersed, finally on the note that everyone would collect on Saturday i.e after three days, at the same time in the staff room, after they've followed up on the action plan.

As the senior professors left for their respective classes, Uma could sense the excitement and thrill pulsating in the faculty members left behind. 'Justice for Janaki' was the new mantra of the day.

That whole day and the next, Uma went about as if on an auto pilot, Janaki's face haunting her every minute of the day. Bereavement, she now realised was such a solitary journey. The pain takes its time to sink in, but once there it eats into you, corroding you deep down till all you are lift with is an agonising abyss of emptiness within you. How her heart grieved for that laughter which had died so young, for that hope which could not see the light of the day, for those unrealised dreams that were snuffed out so cruelly by her very own at every stage of her life, for that woman who wanted so desperately to live, to see her young ones sprout wings and fly in the limitless sky, but was crushed and trampled and trashed away forever.

She was amazed at the reaction and furore her untimely and ugly death had so dramatically created. There were moments when she wondered if Janaki's soul could really see them right now, what would her thoughts truly be? Wouldn't she be surprised to see that all these rich, prominent and powerful women who had never noticed her before, suddenly standing up so ferociously on her behalf, so concerned and obsessed with getting her justice and redressal?

She wondered deeply, at the end of the day, what would 'justice' really man for Janaki?

Every now and then Vatsala's wide eyed face would haunt her too. She often thought about the trauma and grief the poor child had been forced to face because of the one night madness of her own father.

Thursday:

Finally when she could not bear it any longer, Uma took a day off from college and went over to that slum settlement once again. As Uma stood in front of Janaki's house, the realisation of having lost Janaki forever, hit her more forcefully than ever before. She felt her absence more poignantly than she could have ever imagined, gazing at her once happy abode, now so bleak and desolate. If only those walls could express their agony, she felt, they would have wept inconsolably at their bereavement. There was something so forlorn and dreary about the whole place. The Tulsi ka chaura had wilted in the past three days without its mistress and the air was thick with anguish and grief.

As she walked inside, her eyes fell on Janaki's mother-in-law who was grumbling away loudly, "Why don't you also call me God? No one cares about this old blind woman anymore. See I'm so hungry and no one has bothered to serve me lunch till now. They've also taken away my son. Who will run this house now? Who will buy us food?"

Uma quietly handed over the fruits she had got for them. The old woman snatched the whole lot away from her hands and felt each of them urgently and greedily. She then plucked out a banana and stowed away the rest inside her blanket. Peeling off the entire fruit in one go, she ate the banana so lustily that Uma stared at her spellbound. When she was finally through and had licked her fingers to satisfaction, she inquired, "You are the same madam who came when Janaki was unwell, aren't you?" But before Uma could even say yes, Janaki's mother-in-law had started a fresh bout of weeping and ranting. She cursed her son for slaughtering the cow that gave them milk. "You know, my son is a daily wager. Its not that he doesn't earn money, but never as much as Janaki would get from the college. She was a good woman, my daughter-in-law, but she wasn't our kind. Had fancy ideas about books and knowledge. She got Vatsala admitted to a fancy school. Narain was furious with her for that. A wife has no business taking such decisions on her own. Wasting good money on stupid ideas that's what it was. But for all her show of meekness, she was an adamant woman. Very bad quality for a woman I told her, but why would she listen to a blind old woman. Serves her right that Narain beat her everyday." Taking a deep breath, she was silent for a while and then forgetting the presence of her visitor, she mumbled talking to her own self, "Education is not for poor folks like us. A girl has to be ultimately married off. Who would want an educated girl with strange ideas? How would we get dowry for her? Foolish woman! She was a curse to my house. Now my son is in the police station. God knows what they are doing to him? Who will earn for us now? Who will buy food for us?" A fresh bout of weeping ensued.

All this time Uma was wondering where Vatsala could be. She wondered if she had resumed her school again, but looking at the old woman lost in her own lamentations, it didn't seem wise to question her about anyone. The room with its melancholic air was suddenly closing in on her. Uma felt extremely claustrophobic and opened the side window for fresh air. As the view opened, she was stunned to see Vatsala rinsing a whole pile of clothes laboriously. The young motherless girl of fifteen had suddenly grown up into a young woman in a matter of three days. Uma came out and called out to her softly. There was something about Uma that Vatsala associated with her mother. She rushed over to hug her and the moment she hid her face in Uma's bosom, all her pent up emotions surged out. She broke down and cried for the first time after her mother's death. Her body racked with sobs, she cried unabashedly, copiously, bitterly; she cried like there was no hope for life anymore.

Much later when the sobs had subsided a bit, and she could muster the strength to speak, she said hoarsely, "Aunty, I'm sorry for letting Màa and you down, but I won't be going to school anymore. Dadi has ordered me to stay home and take care of all the chores – washing, cleaning, cooking. She says it is the penalty I must pay for having such a weak and foolish mother. She says it is because of her that my father has not come back home from that night itself."

Although it was done unintentionally, Uma noticed that the sheer reference of 'that night' made Vatsala's face go stark white and her body rigid with fright. A shiver ran down her entire body and it seemed as if blood had frozen in her veins. It was so obvious that the trauma of that night must have been haunting her very single minute of the day, their horrors echoing in the dark recesses of her mind. Uma hugged her tight, whispering all the while to forget the past for it was over. But the girl in her embrace had wounds that were raw and deep and a stiffness which betrayed fears and insecurities that she was too scared to expose. Uma held her hands tight and said, "Vatsala, if there's anything of your mother that you have seen in me. If you feel that I truly loved your mother, then please tell me what is it that is bothering you?"

The plea as envisaged had its effect. With a trembling voice that revealed the shyness beneath and a shame that is often woven into such confidences she said haltingly, "Aunty, ever since the day they took my papa away, the policemen have been coming to our house frequently and at all odd times.

Many times they send everyone out of the room and ask me all kinds of questions about my parents and me, which I hate. I do not like the way they stare at me. Aunty, I'm scared. There's one of them who's extremely horrible and he always stands so close to me that I feel like vomiting. He told me today that he will call me to the police station one of these days. Aunty I heard them saying that the college professors are making too much fuss about this case. They've been meeting their seniors, politicians and media, so the pressure has suddenly increased and now they will have to show some more arrests and call some more of us for investigation."

Every word spoken by Vatsala was like a hammer hitting Uma on the head. She could feel the blood draining from her body as she heard the young girl speak about her fears and helplessness. This was how ugly life could be. These were the grotesque realities borne out of the womb of those bewitching causes. Uma believed in ideals, but translating them into actions, bringing 'revolution' is a very tight rope to walk on and many times failures, like conjurers, sadly cause the death of the one they so strive to protect. If only those who were screaming 'Justice for Janaki' knew how fatal that justice could turn out to be.

To Uma's question of how they were managing at home, Vatsala replied, "There is no money at home. That night papa had snatched away all the money maa had for his drinks. All the provision that was at home is over now. I will now have to take on some part time jobs in the apartments nearby. There's a faraway cousin of my mother who owns a tea stall near the railway station. He had been pleading with my mother for a year now, to let my brother Amit work for him. He needs young boys for serving and cleaning. However, my mother would not hear of it. She wanted Amit to study. But when this uncle came home after the death of my mother, Amit insisted on going with him. I let him go Aunty. At least my Uncle will feed him properly and keep him safe. What option do I have for him anyways, without food and money for school?"

Uma's heart bled for this young girl. She had borne more than was possible for anyone to bear. But there was little Uma could do for her right then, except to tell her that she was not alone and that if there was any major problem she should call her without fail on her mobile. She wrote her phone number on a piece of paper and told her to always keep it with her. She slipped some money into her hands with strict advice not to tell anyone about it. Finally with a heavy heart, she left the nearly orphaned girl and came back.

Saturday:

As decided the faculty met in the staff room at the appointed hour. The mood of the five team members was very upbeat and high. Each of them seemed to have been successful in their respective projects. To begin with their Hindi professor Mrs. Rekha Srivastava got up and gave a step by step account of their meeting with the Deputy Commissioner of Police (crime) and the SHO of the Bani Park police station and how they had promised full cooperation and support. Janaki's husband Narain, she told them all, was still in police custody as the court had granted an extension of his custody by another fourteen days. Although after just two days of being denied food and water and a little routine thrashing, he had finally admitted to having beaten his wife to death albeit accidently. The SHO was quite pleased with the development. According to him, their work was practically over and now it was for the judiciary to do the rest.

The news was greeted by the faculty with a thunderous applause. As Rekha sat down with a contented smile, Puja Bhasin got up, cleared her throat and recounted how Madhavi, Rekha and she had met the chairperson of Rajasthan State Commission for Women at their office in Lal Kothi near Tonk Road. The Chairperson had been kind enough to give them full time and attention and was genuinely moved by Janaki's story. She said that they would do everything within their means to ensure justice for Janaki. They then also met the Chairperson of National Commission for Women who incidentally was in Jaipur on Thursday and already knew about this case through the newspapers. She was extremely concerned about the state of women in Rajasthan and the fact that they were being deprived of their rights, discriminated against and subjected to atrocities despite best efforts from the commission to bring in more awareness, encourage gender equality and education for the girl child. She had promised to immediately constitute an inquiry committee which would make spot enquiries, examine witnesses, gather evidences and submit their reports and recommendations as speedily as possible. She promised immediate justice and complete redressal of grievance.

As Puja sat down to another deafening sound of applause, Anita Pratap got up with a stack of newspapers which she spread out on the table for everyone to see. Smugly she informed them how intensively she had the entire case covered in all the local dailies and as small news items in the national dailies too.

She proudly opened the editorial of the leading Hindi daily of Jaipur and said, "I'm sure most of you must have already read my husband Om's editorial on 'Will there be justice for Janaki?' in this paper, which let me inform you all, is the highest circulated paper of any state, in the entire North India. The Wednesday Woman's special supplement has carried my story 'Justice for Janaki' with my bye line. The article has been hailed as a trail blazer by many prominent journalists and the newspaper office has been flooded by letters of appreciation since that day. Then as you can see Om has got his journalist of crime beat to carry out interviews of our principal Mrs. Bose, Chairperson of Rajasthan State Commission Of women and some leading politicians and celebrities on this case in particular and on domestic violence in general."

The faculty was so spellbound by her oration that they even forgot to clap as she sat down. It was after a while when the audience had gathered their wits that they brought the roof down with their cheering. Madhavi gave a secret thumbs up to Anita and she winked back in smug glee.

Madhavi Prakash got up at last and spoke in her loud and clear voice, "I'd like to thank each one of the earlier speaker for their commendable zeal and contribution to this cause. I'd also like to thank Mrs. Rachna Joshi for roping in Mr. Narendra Joshi, the highly renowned criminal lawyer and her husband, to fight the case against Narain without any financial remuneration from Sessions' court onwards. I've personally spoken to Mr. Joshi and he has assured me that with all the eye witnesses and the confession of the accused in our hand; this is truly an open and shut case. Winning it would actually be akin to shooting a sitting duck.

"I'd also like to thank Mrs. Saroj Singh for initiating various campaigns at different levels, for organising the hand bills, posters, placards and banners with the slogan 'Justice for Janaki' and also for procuring candles for the 'Candle Light March' scheduled for today, between 6.30 p.m. and 8.30 p.m. starting from 'Collectorate Circle' to the 'Statue Circle' where we'll all sign a huge bill board and hold a small prayer meeting for the peace of the departed soul. We've incidentally invited some prominent national level activists and celebrities for the Candle Light March to attract more crowds.

"Mrs. Saroj Singh has also taken the initiative to plan out a 'Janaki Insaaf Mahila Morcha' on Monday at 12 noon starting from our college gate to the Chief Minister's office. While on this I'm taking this opportunity to request Mrs. Anita Pratap to kindly arrange for maximum coverage of this protest. It's high time woman got recognised as an equal.

"In the end I'd like to thank each one of you for your full hearted support and conviction in the cause and I assure you that the goal is not far off and 'Justice for Janaki' is just round the corner.

"Before we disperse, kindly repeat after me three times 'Justice for Janaki'."

The slogan was repeated with great gusto followed by a fresh round of applause and a great amount of cheering and bonhomie.

Uma suddenly felt dizzy. She couldn't stand there anymore. The room seemed to be closing in on her. She felt choked and asphyxiated. She had this urge to run out and fill in her lungs with fresh air. Aditi noticed the changing shades of her face and clutched her hand tight, "Uma are you alright?"

Uma couldn't utter a word. Her throat felt parched, her lips dried, her voice frozen.... She looked at Aditi mutely, helplessly, knowing that the battle was already lost. The 'Trojan Horse' had been, so gloriously carried in.

'Justice for Janaki' had been mounted on such a grandiose frame that both the justice and Janaki were lost in its magnificence. Uma's heart bled for Janaki. Where was she in this whole drama? She, who was a woman with simple dreams, a woman for whom those dreams were the only reason for her life, the only purpose of her 'being', for whom no pain was pain enough, no suffering – suffering, as long as there was this rainbow at the end of the desert. She who bore every atrocity, every extremity only because she had one single hope in life, one single ray of sunshine, which bore the promise of a million suns.

They called this 'Justice for Janaki' and she wanted to scream "How?"

Did these saviours have the faintest idea who 'Janaki' was?

They who had never bothered to glance at her direction even once when she was alive, they who had never thought of her as a human being or as a woman as long as she lived. Did they know her longings, her desires, her dreams? How could they suddenly claim to give her what she would have wanted out of life?

Thinking of Janaki brought to her mind kaleidoscopic images of eyes dancing in merriment, of tinkling laughter like a cascade falling in the wilderness, of indomitable joy and hope despite all adversities, of a 'wisdom' which believed that real poverty was not lack of money but lack of knowledge, of a 'compassion' which could see beyond her own victimisation, into the fears and complexes of her oppressors, of a 'childhood' which grew up playing in the vast open spaces of Bikaner, watching shifting sand dunes, sitting under the peepal trees eating ber, amla, imli on the sly and weaving dreams of becoming a teacher one day, standing in front of a blackboard with around thirty students looking at her in awe, and savouring the imaginary thrill of it, of a mother who had dared to weave dreams for her children despite standing unsheltered and vulnerable in the scorching heat of life.

Freedom from her physical suffering was never the driving force for her. She had accepted that part with a larger empathy and equanimity of her heart. The driving force of her life was Vatsala's education and future. That was the fulcrum of all her struggles and endeavours. She desired to live anew through her daughter, to see her own lifeless dreams resurrect again, to feel her crushed longings spring out with new faith and hope. She had been saving secretly for the day when her daughter would be ready to fly high, the day when no paucity of funds would clip her wings or compel Janaki into denying her the chance to be free to seek newer horizons.

In their enthusiasm for justice these saviours had nipped those very wings before they had even learnt to flap. Because of their enthusiasm Narain would now be behind bars for his life. The family would be without money, food, basic necessities. Since Janaki had neither expired on job nor had worked for requisite years, she wasn't eligible to receive financial support from the institution. Justice for these activists, reformists did not entail wanting to look after her undone jobs, to care for her children who were anchorless and defenseless without her, to fulfill her dreams so that her soul could rest in peace. Justice for them meant creating noise, seeking attention, excitement, popularity, fame and revenge. It meant winning their small battles, even if the main war be lost.

Uma could feel bile rising in her throat. She could see the entire act for the sham that it was. There was no way she could be a party to these meetings, *mahila morchas* and the candle light marches anymore. She had to get out of this claustrophobic atmosphere.

Suddenly in that moment of distress, everything seemed so clear to her. There was no confusion anymore. She now knew what she had to do. She got up from her seat with an urgency she had never felt before. She could sense Aditi trying to clutch at her hand and pull her back, but Uma was like a woman possessed, beyond hearing, beyond control. Somewhere at the back of her mind she could hear affronted voices censoring her for leaving so abruptly and then Aditi's soft repartee," Oh please for God's sake. Can't you see how badly she has taken Janaki's demise. I think Uma is quite unwell. Just look at her face. I think I'll have to take her to the Doctor." Uma could hear all these voices echoing, reechoing and revolving in her outer orbits whereas she felt herself, fated to spin and move, on the compulsion of her own convictions.

She walked out with quick steps, scampered and finally ran to the parking lot. She didn't notice Aditi following her on heels and watching her in strange fascination as she switched off the central lock and climbed into the car. She pushed the key in the ignition and as soon as the engine revved up to life, she was off as if in a trance, without noticing that Aditi, too worried to let her be alone in this state, had sneaked in from the back door quietly.

It didn't take her long to reach the slum settlement and parking the car under the shade of the big neem tree just outside the colony, she practically ran in, too eager to waste a second more. The Tulsi ka chaura was bare. Somebody had already thrown away the dried and lifeless plant and to Uma's apprehensive heart it simply symbolised the bleak future of everything associated with Janaki in that house. She yanked off the curtain, rushed inside and looked out frantically for Vatsala. Not seeing her there, she looked out behind the room. As she had imagined Vatsala was sitting behind a stack of utensils, scrubbing them industriously. Uma reached out hurriedly, pulled her up unceremoniously and said firmly and urgently, "Vatsala pack up your clothes, books, all that you want of your mother's belonging. You are leaving this place right now. You'll be staying with me in my house from now on and that's final."

Vatsala looked up her hands full of coconut coir smeared in ash, her eyes wide in amazement, shock and disbelief. It took a couple of minutes for the entire communication to sink in. A couple of minutes when every thought stood still, when the soul brimmed over with relief, gratitude and thankfulness, when the whole universe spun around in beatitude and bliss. A couple of minutes and the young girl was transformed into a child once again, oblivious of the coir, ash and grime and she was hugging Uma, with a fierceness that expressed everything which was beyond her to put into words, with tears flowing from her eyes incessantly, brazenly, unabashedly.

A little distance away Aditi stood watching them, trembling with happiness and elation. Without any pomp and show, without any sound and noise; how beautifully had justice been delivered to Janaki.

✦ ✦ ✦

7

Wind beneath the Wings

It is nine thirty in the night by the time Pallavi maneuvers the car into the drive and switches off the engine. It has been a long tiring day in the office, which is quite usual and a bumper to bumper traffic on the road which is just as usual too. The lights are switched on the entire street outside and the house as well, except for the portion of her living area, the two bedroom set on the right hand side of the big bungalow. Picking up her leather satchel heavy with laptop and extra files, she switches on the automatic lock of her car. Before climbing up the stairs, she checks up her letter box habitually, where a thick envelope awaits her in all patience. She needs no guesses to know where it has come from or what it contains. She is now getting to have an idea, where all her stubbornness and her persistence comes from. Trust Maa to never give up.

Once inside she slips out of her high heeled Aldo pumps and allows the strap of the satchel to slip off her shoulders. Walking into her room she catches a look at herself in the mirror of her wardrobe. A svelte, elegant figure with a wheatish complexion, slightly roundish face, dark kohled eyes so large that they actually dominate her face, eyelashes that curl bewitchingly, crimson lips and dark lustrous hair cascading down her waist; all stare back at her alluringly.

Glancing at her own reflection, Pallavi has this queer feeling that she is actually watching a stranger. This woman in a fawn shirt and coffee coloured Zara trousers, bewitchingly wrapped in the subtle fragrance of Estee Lauders, is eons away from the one she had known five years back.

She remembers that simple, wide eyed, lively girl of Allahabad five years back, the girl who still lives somewhere in a corner of her heart, the girl who speaks to her in endless moments of her solitude, the girl who desires, dreams, questions and seeks, the girl who craves for her roots secretly and feverishly.

Looking back she feels, 'We do not leave anything behind in life, not even the places and the times we have lived in. They are present in us all the time, walking with us silently every step of our way, hidden in the dark recesses of our mind, camouflaging as memories untold.'

As she peers into the mirror more intently, she sees a young girl in two pigtails, her eyes bright and fiery, with passion for life leaping out like wanton flames, standing in a closed dressing room in front of a similar mirror declaiming the speech of Benito Mussolini justifying his attack on Ethiopia. She sees the girl throwing out her arms to emphasise her words and rouse the emotions of her imaginary audience. The girl is doing this in one of those lazy afternoons when she knows her Maa would be deep into her siesta and would not be able to forbid her from taking part in the annual contest of her school. Often she wonders why there have always been two sets of rules for the two children of the same family. Bhaiyya, her younger brother is egged on and cheered for every little effort, most of which are anyways forced on him, whereas she has to beg, grovel, struggle and sometimes cheat for every little opportunity, every inch of her way. She remembers how they had all gone so enthusiastically for Bhaiyya's school play in which he was a newspaper vendor with about a minute's appearance on the stage. Papa and Maa were so proud of him, so was she but then her reasons were entirely different. Bhaiyya was always her little baby and she glowed in all his achievements, big or small.

In the mirror the girl is now standing with a trophy in her hand, her eyes sparkling with the thrill of achievement, her heart oscillating between the euphoria of victory and an incredulity that it could actually be true, lips parted in joy and half laughter, jubilant with the thrill of being awarded the 'Best Speaker' of the school.

Somewhere in that bliss is also a glimmer of satisfaction for having noticed that look of half smile and half elation in Maa's eyes when she had dramatically pulled the trophy out for her to admire. The ice that is perennially frozen in her eyes melts and the girl sees a river shimmering underneath, flowing and gushing with a warmth she had never witnessed before. That above all to her, is her real victory.

She has always seen a strange anxiety lurking in Maa's eyes, an unknown panic breathing in her every second of the day. Fear it seemed was the unidentified fifth member of the family who lived with them unseen, unaddressed.

Bowing to Papa's diktat has been the one single parameter for the approval of their existence. He does not raise his voice, does not show aggression, yet he manages to create terror with his cold looks and clipped tone. This terror can send shivers down one's spine. It stifles her.

The image with the trophy fades out and a new one takes shape. The girl is sitting in her school, filling out the form for her elective subjects. She had been advised to opt for humanities, despite her brilliant performance in all subjects, simply because she has an aptitude for languages especially creative writing. She secretly craves to be a writer, but is adamant to choose science. Her closest friend Vidhi has opted for English, Psychology and Home Science. There is no one she could turn to for guidance. She is scared if she opts for humanities Papa would get her married off as soon as she completes her graduation. She feels like a bird in captivity. She must fly off before they clip her wings. She must be economically free.

She is frightened, she is scared. This to her is the only way out of the maze of life. Fear is hounding her. She can feel it sneaking up to her in silent measured steps slowly, stealthily. She would not let it pounce on her; she would not let it enter her house.

Now in the mirror she is standing in her new salwar kameez, nervous. Today is her first day in 'all girls college'. There are no co-educational Degree colleges under their state University which is just as well, for she knows papa would have never allowed her to join one in any case. Maa, it seems, has already been instructed to make sure that her dresses are simple and sober. Pallavi has been explicitly instructed to go straight to college from home and back again, in her college bus with no detour whatsoever and that any bunking of class, spending money or time in canteen would lead to serious repercussions. She is anyway too nervous and scared to defy them.

She sees herself entering the portals of that institution with a sense of amazement and awe. There are many others around like her, diffident, nervous, controlled by invisible threads at home, yet pulsatingly alive to the many splendoured promises of the future ahead.

The vision fades into another one, this time the girl is sitting in the last bench of her college bus glued into this incredibly powerful book on existentialism. Vidhi has introduced her to the world of books, a world where she can travel around anywhere, without anyone suspecting, much less forbidding her, where she can feel and experience new emotions fearlessly, unabashedly. Vidhi hands her over the choicest books of known, unknown authors and poets and Pallavi devours them greedily, hungrily assimilating all that is cerebrally enriching and enlightening. Sometimes she scribbles random thoughts arising either out of sudden surge of emotions or at times out of deep contemplations, thoughts that create a path for her journey within herself. Her articles and poems make their way into the college magazine and over the time she is nominated for the editorial board. Her article on 'youth power' gets chosen for a special debate on the All India Radio station. The principal arranges for her to go along with their HOD for the recording. She thinks of papa and breaks out in cold sweat, however there is no way she can refuse the principal. Although once there in front of the mike, everything else fades out except her passion and her single minded drive to give out her best. She speaks with all her intensity and conviction and is declared a winner with a certificate and cheque of five thousand rupees. She is in tears thinking about the wrath she would have to face at home. Luckily the principal calls papa and congratulates him profusely, praising him for his daughter's exemplary conduct and her talents. This makes it easier at home although papa does not fail to mention that since it was the principal who made her defy his orders, he is overlooking the matter this once; but that he still stands by each of his rules laid out for her.

Little does anyone know that this would prove to be the first step in her fairly long and interesting journey into this fascinating world of audio media! It begins with a talk or two, going on to discussions, poetry recitals, interviews, plays, anchoring and news reading on a casual basis. The most comforting aspect of this otherwise risky adventure being that owing to papa's dislike for wasting time on entertainments like radio, no one gets to learn about her escapades.

Yet another image shimmers in the mirror. She is confiding in Vidhi that she would not be applying for medical pre entrance. Her heart is just not into it. Vidhi is looking on incredulously, "Pallavi, what's wrong with you? You went against everyone and opted for Science and now this. Why?"

Her eyes are now filling out with tears. Suddenly she is the little lost, nine years old girl, unsure of herself, scared of her father's displeasure at her conduct. She so wants to please him, yet she wonders why is it always so difficult? It should be so easy for any daughter to fall in line with his choices and desires, for doing so demands the least effort; yet why has it always been so difficult for her? What is it that she is seeking so desperately? Why must the path she choose, always be so tortuous, so arduous?

She is unhappy, restless, confused. She does not desire to rebel yet she cannot be untrue to herself too. She sees her other friends either falling in line with their parents and buying peace or manipulating them to get what they want. She can do neither of the two for she essentially needs to be honest and to be herself at all cost.

Image shifts and now she is poring over the newspaper, tense, nervous and skeptical. The result for the MBA entrance for the Management Institute of the University has been declared. After much deliberation she had decided to take this route to achieve her goal of independence and empowerment. She has worked extremely hard for it learning new subjects, mastering those she had never had any inclination for like Maths and Statistics. She has been like a soul possessed for the last eight months and today was the D day.

Suddenly she sees it. Her roll number out there smiling and winking at her. She stares at it spellbound for two whole minutes. She wants to make sure this is real. She wants to hold on to this moment, to feel it, to savour this sensation of incredible delight and ecstasy. And then as soon as the reality starts making some sense, she lets out a yell loud enough to bring the whole house down.

This was not what papa had planned for her, but he is wise enough to flow with the events and let destiny takes its own course. With bhaiyya having got into a prestigious engineering college, he is of late quite relaxed and in a more congenial frame of mind. Maa as usual is undecipherable. She appears detached, her eyes betraying no emotions, yet Pallavi can sense the elation effervescing inside her. And she wonders if that is what the umbilical cord is all about. This connection which transcends both speech and expression and nurtures the child in us, defying all concept of age, distance and logic. Somewhere deep inside, she is infused with the feeling of floating, in the warmth and comfort of the amniotic fluid all over again.

The vision changes abruptly. She is now pacing up and down the length of her room, fuming, seething with fury, simmering with frustration. Why don't they let her be? Why must she fight every inch of her way, every day in her life? Why must her gender overshadow everything else that there is to her? Oh Why?

She has been picked up by sole distributors of a leading pharmaceutical company six months back, under the campus placement programme. Her job requires her to take delivery of the pharmaceutical products and supervise the printing of advance invoices that may be presented in the bank the first thing next morning. This way her firm receives payment the same time as its own becomes due to the supplying company.

Her job profile, therefore, needs her to be in the office on certain days of the month till quite late in the evening. The office incidentally is walking distance from home. Yet there is so much problem on this issue nearly every day. Most of the times when she is late home she tiptoes inside like a thief, like a culprit and hates herself for doing so. The entire act makes her feel so small, so pathetic.

Today again there is another scene. As it happens, there has been a fresh viral epidemic in the state and the quantity of drugs received and dispatched exceeded the regular quantity by a phenomenal amount. So it was nearly 9.30 p.m. by the time she could come home. Maa was standing at the door and had declared the ultimatum that 'enough was enough'. "We have tolerated your willfulness for quite some time now. We live in a society where people question us on the reason for such blatant liberty to our daughter. You wanted to do MBA and we allowed you to do so, against our better judgement and desire. You wanted to work, we bowed down again, so that once you are married and gone, you will have no regrets, no complaints. But now this is going too far. People are talking about your late hours. A girl's name is the most fragile thing ever. It takes very little to break it. Who do you think will marry you if your name is tarnished so?"

Pallavi stands transfixed. She is speechless. She cannot believe what she is hearing. This is taking the entire issue too far. Oh, the unfairness of it all. Most of the boys in their neighbourhood and community work till late nights. They even party late nights after office hours, but that is fine with everybody. And here she has been going from home to office and back again, working hard, trying to learn and grow and she is to be labeled a bad girl. Oh really? Bhaiyya too works late hours, goes on tours, parties the night through. But that's fine. No one ever says a word to him. So why her?

She is not a baby. She knows that every word that her maa has spoken, has come from papa. Maa is always the voice. Would she too become like her one day? Just a name, a face, a voice? Just a mask, a cover, a veil? Every fiber of her being revolts at such a prospect. She needs to run away somewhere, anywhere and soon.

She is pacing faster, much faster, the fury inside her working itself up to a crescendo. Oh, the sheer duplicity of it all. Wrath and resentment leap up like flames consuming her like a jungle fire, razing all that is meek and subservient in her, all that is pliant and unquestioning in her, to ashes.

The images fade into another one.

Now she is standing in front of a mirror checking herself out nervously in a luxury hotel in Delhi. She is here with her senior Director to meet the CEO of a leading cosmetic company for a marketing presentation. She is now the Advertising Manager of a leading newspaper in Delhi.

It has been an year since she has shifted here from Allahabad and she owes this feat to bhaiyya who requested the PRO of his company, also a very good friend of his, to tap her contacts and see if something could be worked out for his sister. Thus on the pretext of staying with bhaiyya for a few days, Pallavi manages to sneak out to the Capital brimming with excitement and hope. She so wants to try out her luck in this city which has been known to make 'dreams come true' for those who believe in themselves.

But if she had thought that with her management degree, her extracurricular activities, experience and knowledge, she stood a fighting chance, then Delhi shows her that she needs to think again. If anything she has learnt how ruthless and arrogant the job market can be. Also that it is the packaging and not the content that sells. The PRO had handed her over a list of names of all those she closely knew in the advertising agencies and the newspaper industry; whom she could go and meet. The rest, she had said depended on Pallavi's own efforts and luck.

Armed with her qualifications and other relevant documents, she had walked enthusiastically, doggedly, relentlessly from office to office, sitting outside for hours together waiting to be called in for an interview, at times lasting for only two minutes, going without food for the entire day for she needed to cover as much as possible in those few days. Finally it was at this newspaper office that she was interviewed by the Director marketing, a hawk eyed man of a fairly advanced age, who also happened to be, as she learnt much later, a father of four daughters. And as he confessed afterwards, it was her simplicity, her intensity and passion for work that swung the needle in her favour in the first meeting itself.

There is a lot of resistance from maa and papa regarding her shift to Delhi. They want to get her married off at the earliest and fail to understand this nonsense about job, career and empowerment. Vidhi had got married a few months back and that for them should have been a signal for her to follow suit. But bhaiyya stands in her favour like a rock. Finally thinking that roughing out away from the comfort of the family would bring her back to their fold in no time, they relent with a condition that she may have her way for one year at the most, by the end of which they would get her married anyways.

It is not easy for her to get along in the harshly competitive world of the newspaper industry. If she had expected her female colleagues to be warm, congenial and kind, then she had another think coming. Day after day, she faces arrogance, sarcasm, humiliation, as much for her qualifications which they secretly envied, as for her obvious ignorance about the print media. But she does not let it faze her. She has her entire future at stake, which these girls with half their knowledge than hers, half their commitment, resilience, steel than hers could never understand. She isn't arrogant, but herself – respect is non-negotiable and she has to prove that. She requests her boss to send her out in the field with their star marketing executive, a woman who carries herself like a celebrity and of whom everyone in the office is openly in awe of.

Permission received, she follows her mentor like a little lamb, doing all her paperwork, covering up for her occasional indiscretions and admiring her unabashedly which wins her all the affection in return. Within a month she has built up a rapport and a trust that urges her senior to teach her everything there is about the work, her personal strategy and the competition. She gives Pallavi all the important tips on grooming and presentation too. The packaging it seems is essential to the product, no matter what the worth.

The girl standing in front of the mirror checking herself out nervously in a luxury hotel walks out of the meeting a couple of hours later smiling smugly, comfortable in the knowledge that she has the new campaign, the CEO of the cosmetic company and her Director wrapped up neatly in her bag. There is a spring in her step, a smile in her eyes and a look about her which says, "I am ready to take on the world."

Each vision in the mirror brings in waves of memories whooshing and swirling around her. She finds herself flowing in their tide, bobbing to their motion and surrendering to their spell, in absolute trance. She stands mesmerised in front of these surging waves of reminiscences, and would have continued to do so but for the ringing of her phone which shakes her out of the deep reverie. It is Vidhi. It normally is her at this time of the day, when she knows that Pallavi would be home, after work, tired and alone.

There is something very strange about your close friends, especially the ones you've grown up with. They're like your second self, like the breath you draw in every moment oblivious to its essentiality in your life, like the blood flowing in your veins, like the heart pumping in your body. Much as you may desire, there is nothing you can ever hide from them. They can read your silences just as lucidly as they can see the inner darkness shrouded behind your bright smile.

Pallavi recalls how Vidhi and she had been together since they had been in First standard. For a number of years in the beginning, till Pallavi's father could get the government bungalow, they had been neighbours too and so had practically grown up together. They had learnt their first alphabets together, broken their baby teeth around the same time, played with dolls, skipped rope, climbed trees and giggled together nonstop. They had played silly pranks, told harmless lies to cover up for each other, helped each other with home assignments, projects, and shared growing up fears, excitement and frustrations. They had shared their moments of ecstasies, their most secret sorrows, hurts caused by misunderstandings, anguish over broken friendships and all the trivia that appears to be a matter of life and death in those tender teen years along with their aspirations and dreams with each other and had promised to always-always stay in touch, no matter what. They had honoured their intention and guarded their friendship most zealously and reverently.

Vidhi, a lecturer and now a mother of two years old daughter Nandini, had been married to a Marketing professional in Mumbai for the last five years, where she lived with her parents-in-law, struggling to meet the norms of an ideal daughter-in-law, wife and mother, all together, under all kinds of circumstances, every day.

Her infrequent calls to Pallavi and vice versa, has been the only sphere where she has managed to keep some personal space, in her otherwise completely distributed life.

Their talks range from inane matters to the most profound ones. And Pallavi often thinks amusingly, if ever questioned, she would find it extremely difficult to remember what they had actually talked about in their entire one hour's session, yet this one conversation refueled their energies for the next five to six days, recharging them with an inexplicable joy and delight.

This time round, it was Vidhi's patter which reached across the silence between them enveloping Pallavi in her disarming affection, artlessness and spontaneity. Starting from her Nandini's comical antics, to her maid's problems, her sister-in-law's unannounced weekend visit, to Nikhil her husband asking her to take a day off from the college for amma's check-up for Glaucoma, the topics she covered seemed endless. Pallavi listening indulgently, could feel the warmth of their bond, coursing down her entire being, running through her veins right into her heart, rushing out to every cell of her body, infusing a sense of well being and an irrepressible desire to giggle like she would when they were in their early teens. Pallavi found herself bantering her about the wisdom of marrying early and teasing her playfully, "Serves you right for ditching me for the first handsome man your parents lined up for you." She could see Vidhi giggling at this rejoinder, at the other end of the phone, much before she could hear the sound.

"Oh yeah! And what about your handsome one darling? Don't tell me you're not thinking about marriage yourself?"

Pallavi could feel blood rushing to her ears at this rejoinder. Trust Vidhi to give it back as good as she got it. She felt a nervous laughter rising in her throat and was sure that Vidhi too must have heard the loud thumping of her heartbeats, just as clearly, miles away. Deftly changing the subject, she barged on to other topics like that latest movie everyone has been so talking about, the book of Rumi which she had couriered to Vidhi just a day before and the book fair that she was planning to visit that very weekend.

Yearning to hear as much as possible, to say as much as they could, it took them another half an hour to reluctantly wind up their conversation, with a promise to catch up with each other again after two days.

The cheer that such calls invariably generated, made Pallavi conscious of just how ravenous she was suddenly feeling, having had to forego her lunch for a very important presentation that afternoon. She peeped into the kitchen to see what Maya her maid had cooked for her that night. The appetising aroma wafting out of the casseroles disclosed fresh tomato soup with palak paneer, mixed raita and dal just the way maa made it. Pallavi sent a silent thanksgiving for Maya who had been such a find and the very thought of what she would ever do without her, made her shudder involuntarily.

Maya had come to her in a three foolscap sheets of a letter from Vidhi wherein she had explained how she had rescued Maya, from being sold off to a brothel, along with the Social Service League of her college. On making detailed inquiries they found out that she hailed from Kakori near Lucknow. Her parents had been murdered in a family feud a couple of years back when she had just completed her High School. Her father's elder brother under the guise of her guardianship had taken possession of their land and property and after two years of unrelenting slavery at home had sold her off to a pimp under the pretense of marriage. The pimp had brought her to Mumbai where she was handed over to a woman running a brothel, who submitted her to unspeakable tortures to break her into submission. Yet the girl kept up her resistance with all her might. However the Social Service League of their college was tipped off by one of their informers and they were able to save Maya from a future worse than death. Vidhi had mentioned that there was something so pitiful and helpless in that's girl's eyes which stirred all the maternal instincts in her.

Vidhi had written, "It's so strange Pallavi, but being a mother to Nandini has made me a mother to every child, every vulnerable soul in this universe, if you can understand what I mean. Now I realise that being a mother is not a function of the womb. It is in fact all about your heart. There was no way I could hand her over to a women relief center where I would always be worried about her safety and future."

Vidhi wondered if Pallavi could keep her as a maid giving her home and affection while allowing her to complete her studies through correspondence. Pallavi mulled over the idea for over a week, but in the end, she was convinced that it did seem sensible, viable and attractive.

Thus Maya had come to Delhi and Pallavi loved her in the first meeting itself. Maya however was like a wounded dove in the beginning, very scared and nervous. The demons within her were too powerful for Pallavi to try and exorcise them. So she just decided to let her be. Nothing heals a wounded spirit better than a whole lot of space, silence and solitude. All she chose to give unstintingly was her warmth and understanding.

Gradually the ice melted, gradually life flowed in the frozen blood streams again, gradually the eyes smiled and gradually, she hoped, those eyes would learn to laugh again. Pallavi was willing to wait for that day, no matter how long the journey.

Meanwhile she offered her the other room, arranged for her necessities, some new clothes and got her enrolled in the graduation course of IGNOU. After the first few months of living as family, with no jobs assigned, no expectations made, Pallavi saw Maya expressing willingness to share the work load and being happy in making substantial contribution of her own. Basically a hard working girl, she was already used to handling all the chores alone in her uncle's house, specially cooking which she found very therapeutic. As the time passed Maya took to running the house independently and Pallavi treating her as a member of the family, allowed her to take her own decisions in her work area. She also helped her open up her own account and deposit her monthly salary into it regularly. This gave her a sense of self worth, a sense of independence and confidence. Over the time an unspoken bond grew between the two. Over the time the healing took place, although Pallavi knew that the scars would be there as long as she lived.

Devouring her late dinner, she was happy to have issued instructions that under no conditions must Maya stay awake for her to come home. She was happy to have conveyed that she prefers to be by herself while unwinding and equally happy to have insisted that Maya's priority must be to excel in her studies and become independent in due course of time.

This absolved her of any possibility of guilt for making her stay up late or hungry or both while waiting for her.

Much later in the night while going through 'Signs of the Unseen' by Rumi her thoughts wandered over her conversation with Vidhi, most specifically her innocent query, "And what about your handsome one darling? Don't tell me you're not thinking about marriage yourself?"

The handsome one? Well, Nagesh Krishnan was anything but handsome, yet there was something about him which made Pallavi's heart miss a beat every time he strode into the room, something that made her knees turn to jelly every time he smiled at her tenderly, something that made her feel effervescent and dizzy every time he laughed aloud, something that tied up her stomach in knots every time he stood close enough for her to be able to smell his after shave, something that made her want to die every time he held her in his arms.

Thinking of Nagesh took her back to that meeting her Director had fixed up in the former's conference room on one December Sunday which also happened to be her birthday. Since she was by now the unofficial lieutenant to her Director, her own mentor, having chosen marriage to her childhood love over her job, it was understood that Pallavi would be the one making the presentation on the Director's behalf. As it was, all the collating of the data, analysing, preparing slides complete with statistical data and pie charts was her own initiative. Normally she looked forward to these presentations and treated each of them as a fresh challenge to her knowledge and convincing skill. But this once she was indescribably furious at this unknown client, the Vice President of the company which happened to be the market leader of the electronics industry.

A man according to Pallavi, who was so self centered and arrogant as to ruin her Sunday and more so her birthday for his own whim and fancy.

As their car approached the Corporate Office, the view of the imposing building, the lush green lawns, the warm winter sun and the pure fresh air took her breath away and she resented this majorly for she desperately wanted to hold on to her displeasure at being so summoned by this 'high and mighty' client.

Inside his office they were met courteously by his Assistant Manager marketing, who escorted them immediately to their equally plush and state of art conference room. This was where her eyes fell on Nagesh Krishnan, the Vice President of the leading electronics company for the first time.

Sitting at the head of the table with his team of five senior managers, he was deeply engrossed in drafting their new promotion strategy. There was an aura of authority and strength about him, which suddenly made her nervous despite all her attitude about her poise and confidence. As soon as he became aware of their presence, he stood up and walked up to her Director, in deference to his age and seniority (which she was to learn much later), with the most disarming smile Pallavi had ever seen. There was something absolutely electric about this tall, broad shouldered man which mesmerised her completely. A man in early forties with refreshingly clean shaven look, a pleasant demeanour, a gentle smile that reached his eyes and an aura of authority which he wore with absolute ease; Nagesh was someone like she had never ever met before. She saw him as if in a trance, apologising to her Director for having spoiled their Sunday, but since he had to finalise the new campaign before his trip to France and since he had promised to give them an audience, he had no other option available to him.

Against her sturdiest resolve, Pallavi could feel her anger melting away at his spontaneous warmth and openness. Introductions over, she plunged into her presentation with all conviction and gusto. Normally when she ended up her delivery, she was used to having her audience completely smitten, sold and eating out of her hands for her in depth knowledge and incisive study. But this once she was in for a surprise. Nagesh asked her the most penetrating questions, which showed her clearly that he was an expert both in market research and the newspaper industry. Layer by layer he peeled off all that was non-essential and exaggerated in her presentation, leaving the basic facts bare and open for them to see. In the end however, he did agree that their publication could definitely help his brand to address the target audience, he had in his mind.

By the time they were done, it was quite late. So he requested them to join him for tea. Within minutes a spread was laid out for them, which reminded her how famished she was, having foregone her breakfast and lunch both in fury and stress. Before they could start, his assistant wheeled in an exotic cake with a single candle shimmering gloriously. Nagesh announced to his team in his easy drawl, "This, my friends, is with our sincere apologies to the lovely lady out here, whose birthday was hijacked by us inadvertently."

Pallavi could have died of embarrassment and joy at the same time, not knowing whether to laugh or cry at that moment. It must have been her Director who had let the cat out of the bag. Despite her best efforts, she blushed to her roots like a fifteen years old. All through their tea, Nagesh was attention personified, gracious, kind, yet impersonal. There was none of the desire for familiarity, which so irritated her in other clients. As she left his office that day, she realised that for the first time ever in her life she had fallen for someone's charms hook, line and sinker.

The campaign as promised came through in due course and they never had any reason to meet or interact again after that. Nagesh Krishnan was slowly set aside in her mind as an interesting and exciting memory which made her feel wistful at times for reasons unknown.

After a few months of this meeting, her Director retired and a new one from another organisation was brought in to take charge. The new guy walked in with a prefixed agenda of bringing in his own team into this organisation. So in the coming months, he took every opportunity to belittle and humiliate Pallavi for no reason at all. She tried her best to earn his respect and prove her worth, but when it became clear to her, that defeat in this battle was a foregone conclusion, she started looking for a change.

It was then that she saw the advertisement for a Corporate Communication Manager in Nagesh's company. Thinking that he probably must have forgotten all about her, she applied immediately. Her interview was conducted by a panel and she was short listed for the final meeting with the Vice President. As she walked into his chamber, every fiber in her body was screaming at her to turn around and run. But then there are times in life when you have to simply allow yourself to flow with the current, when you can see your destiny taking you right where it wants you to be and there is nothing you can do to prevent it.

Seeing him for the second time in a much more official setting made her heart jump to her mouth, her palms cold, sweaty, her lips dry and for a minute she felt like her lungs had forgotten to breathe. She noticed a flicker of recognition in his eyes as he looked up, but the very next moment she wondered if she had imagined it.

If she had thought that he would question her on her reasons for leaving her earlier job or for choosing an entirely different line altogether, she was in for a surprise. He told her briefly about his brand and his vision for it in the coming years. As he spoke, Pallavi noticed his single minded focus, his intensity, his command on the language, his economy of words and his deep bass voice so smooth and silky that it tingled her spine and made her come alive in a million ways. So by the time he asked her about her vision for herself and where exactly she sees herself in the next five years, Pallavi could speak with a comfort, ease and a fervour that matched his, about self actualisation and self empowerment. As they conversed, she was completely surprised to see their mental and emotional compatibility on nearly all issues and so was unfazed when he finally offered her the job.

Deep in her reverie, the book of Rumi still in her hands, her thoughts go back to absolute exhilaration of that moment when she had finally held the appointment letter in her hand. It had indeed been a dream-come-true. There was lots to learn as the Corporate Communications Manager of an electronics company and the coming months saw her passionately plunging into this task. She was invariably the first to arrive and the last to leave, going through all their past work, their market information and sitting up after office hours with the executives of their advertising agency to understand their processes and functions. Many a time she would be aware of Nagesh walking past by her cabin with a cursory glance at her deep into her work.

This was incidentally, also the time, when bhaiyya was sent on an overseas assignment to Paris and she had grabbed the opportunity to find herself a fully furnished two bedroom annexe in Panchsheel Enclave. Maa had come over under the guise of supervising the arrangement of Pallavi's kitchen, to assure herself of the suitability of her new abode. Papa's invisible presence behind maa was once again so vividly obvious to her. She further went ahead and bought herself a new car under the company car lease scheme.

Then came the time to launch an entirely new state-of-the-art product into the market that had required her to interact much more closely and frequently with Nagesh for the next few months. They would both often end up working late with the marketing team and the agency and finally he would insist on ordering dinner before dropping her home himself. Such concern coming from a man as senior as him, especially when his work load was far more phenomenal than hers, would humble and overwhelm her no end. Sitting in his office over dinner, or next to him in the car and unwinding after a hard day's work, talking to him about their mutual passion for books, about David Lean films, about Mrinal Sen, Bimal da, about Girija Devi, Kishori Amonkar, Ajoy Chakroborty, she realised how similar they both actually were deep down. Despite all this, she guarded her emotions and expressions almost ferociously, for she figured that it was easy for a single girl to be misunderstood at the drop of a hat.

Yet the chemistry couldn't be denied and she could see Nagesh slowly warming up and responding to it. Over the time he sought her company more often and even took to confiding official problems that she knew he wouldn't dream of, with anyone else. She could feel their relationship evolving with time from that of a boss and subordinate, to that of closest friends and maybe a little more, but they both shied of facing it for reasons of their own.

Their new product launch entailed press conferences, dealers' conferences, dinners, events and tours to every state. It was during one such tour that Pallavi got up in her room feeling dizzy and nauseous. She was supposed to join Nagesh and their local marketing team for a breakfast meeting at 9 a.m., but she just could not move an inch due to the excruciating body ache and fatigue. Her throat felt scratchy and sore and all she wanted to do was curl up and sleep. She could feel herself sinking into the soft, silky darkness that cradled her gently. Slowly she felt herself sliding away still further into deeper layers of subconscious zone. Somewhere above she could hear the telephone ringing, but it was such a faint voice coming from miles away; then the knocking at the door, at first gently, then louder and louder and then finally a click. Now she was being shaken up, she tried to open her eyes. Oh Nagesh, she smiled stupidly and closed her eyes again.

It was much later in the night that she felt life creeping into her again. She stirred, opened her eyes slowly and saw a soft glow in the room. It took her a minute to realise that she was in the hotel room and had probably slept the entire day. Nagesh who was working on his laptop on a couch close by, sensed the movement and was by her side in an instant. He touched her forehead to check the fever, but it seemed to have subsided for the time being. Pallavi was surprised to see the stress and anguish in his eyes and that haggard look which she could read so clearly even beneath his suave appearance. He sat down near her bed with a lassitude that seemed to have finally taken its toll on him. He then clasped her hand in both of his, bringing his forehead down to it, closing his eyes as if to release the pain within. In an instant all the love within her, welled up in her eyes, all her defenses crumbled down and a sob caught itself in her throat. He looked up, saw the unspoken in him mirrored on her face and before she knew; she was in his arms, close to his chest held so fiercely, so intensely like a drowning man holding on to his last breath. All that she had suppressed so forcibly within her, all that she had denied herself to feel, all that she had dared not dream for fears unknown; exploded in that one instant and tears poured out freely, brazenly, unabashedly. Before she could realise his lips had sought hers, gently at first and then boldly, possessively, passionately.

This was such bliss! She felt like she was floating in heaven. This was such a sweet death; this was such a sweet resurrection.

Much, much later however, she saw him pacing up and down the room fighting with himself, upset and distraught. She begged him to say something and he finally confessed in a broken voice, "I'm so sorry honey. I shouldn't have allowed this to happen. This is just so wrong."

"What's so wrong about love Nagesh?"

"Oh Pallavi, I'm married with two daughters. I had no business falling in love like that. But watching you walk into my conference room, so heated up and annoyed, made me fall head over heels for you. I needed all my strength to steel myself against your liveliness, your charms and your innocence and finally when I thought you were out of my life, you crashed into it again and how. God knows, how I've struggled with my own feelings, how I've fought it every single day, working with you, talking to you, laughing with you, holding it all back in the deepest recesses of my heart."

Pallavi walked up to him, softly embracing him, letting her wordlessness say it all for her. Her joy in his existence, her absolute surrender, and her faith in this beautiful love they had found in each other. In that one moment suspended in timelessness, she had lived a complete life of ecstasy and exaltation.

Despite all his resolve, Nagesh too couldn't fight the surging passions within and they soon found ways and means to get away for a weekend, or a day to be together in their own world of joy.

Pallavi often recalled the early days of her life, the restrictions, the chains, the bondages that her mother and she had lived with. She thought of the fifth unidentified member in their home, the fear; fear she had so hated and abhorred, fear that she had pledged to herself would never sneak up to her, stalk her or pounce on her ever in her life, fear that she had struggled all her life to overcome.

She had dreamt of equality, empowerment, liberation; to be a feeling, thinking human being and not just a body, a voice, a name, a shadow of the other person called 'man'.

She felt glad that she had strived for it relentlessly, that she had earned it with all her courage and resilience, that she had not chosen the easy way out.

She thought of Vidhi, of all her glorious dreams of a perfect life, of all those lofty ideals of existentialism and freedom of Sartre, Ayn Rand, Maya Angelou and finally the harsh reality. She thought of all the compromises that Vidhi had to make every day in the name of values, goodness, duty and traditions, all the tears that she was forced to swallow to buy peace and match the expectations of those around her.

Looking at her and so many of them around her, she bristled, why being a woman was akin to becoming a cattle for you to be branded, stamped and owned by those who claimed their rights on you? Why being a woman robbed you of your very right to breathe free, to make your own choices, your own decisions? Why was a woman handed over in a marriage, gifted as a piece of property in unknown hands to be masters of her life forever?

She thought of Maya and how her gender made her an easy target for anyone to prey on. How her birth as a woman marred her life forever, making her a piece of flesh to covet, to devour, to abuse and trash away. She thought of all the agonies that the poor mite had to bear for her vulnerability as a woman and a shiver ran down her spine in revulsion and horror.

Pallavi had fought against this with every ounce of her strength, annoying her parents, antagonising close relatives, yet unrelenting in her stand. She had been duped into meeting any number of prospective grooms under the guise of friends or connections she didn't know about, but the sixth sense in her almost always sensed their game half way through, leading to fresh bouts of temper at both ends.

Although the only time she ever felt guilty for doing so was during this Diwali when papa had invited Raghav's family over for dinner. They had been close family friends and Raghav, his younger sister, bhaiyya and she would often play 'I spy you', 'Sitolia' or cricket during summer vacations. But as they grew up they got lost into their own maze of school, friends, interests and ultimately careers. Raghav had gone on to do Mechanical Engineering from IIT Delhi followed by management course from a premier institution and was now working for a leading automobile company in Gurgaon. It was therefore not very surprising when papa slyly suggested, "Raghav why don't you and Pallavi get together in Delhi or Gurgaon sometimes. I'm sure you'd both love each other's company." Pallavi could have screamed with exasperation. Why must papa be so blatant?

It was so embarrassing, not to mention so unpalatable to her in the current scheme of things. How she wanted to tell maa about Nagesh and their love for each other, but she just couldn't. Her eyes stung with unshed tears of misery and pain. Why must the only ecstasy in her life be so surreptitious and clandestine? Why should she be denied the joy to announce to one and all, the only relationship which has added meaning to her life, has filled her with infinite bliss, which spoke of her highest values reflected in someone else?

She wondered 'Why was it so wrong to have loved? Love is never planned, it happens to you, it strikes you when you least expect it, transforming you completely and irrevocably. Love can never be governed, it governs you. It is the integrated response of our body, mind and soul, of our thoughts, emotions and vision, of our belief, faith, love and sexual desires. It is the most beautiful and perfect tribute to our ideals.

She was not a home breaker. In fact she desired nothing else but to give unstintingly, unconditionally, unendingly.

This was sufficient for her to be drenched in the showers of love, to feel the joy in every fiber, in every cell. Sufficient for her to know that the air she was breathing in has been touched by her lover too, the night she holds to her bosom at this end, gently caresses him to sleep at the other. Sufficient to know that even if she does not get to see him so often, he exists. And in that existence is her exaltation of life.

Her eyes heavy with sleep, she places her book on the bedside and smiles tenderly at the thought of meeting Nagesh the next morning. It has been a fortnight since he has left for an intensive marketing tour of Chandigarh and Punjab. His absence always creates a vacuum which leaves her feeling choked and asphyxiated. She lives for the moments when she could see him, even if from afar, even if in a crowd, even if immersed in his work oblivious of her. Lost in his thoughts, she never realises when she dozes away into the bliss of deep slumber.

It isn't until next evening that she gets to see Nagesh walking into the office with a pot bellied, nattily dressed man of medium height, graying hair neatly parted and combed, a rope of a gold chain resting proudly on his chest. From the distance that she is, she could see Nagesh tilting his head, saying something to the man at which the latter lets out a bellow of full throated laughter, with Nagesh joining him at a much lower decibel.

Pallavi is amazed to see Nagesh in such an incongruent company seemingly enjoying it too. At around 8 p.m., when she is about to call it a day, Nagesh calls up to tell her that he would like her to join him for dinner at one of the premium luxury hotels in about an hour. His car is available for her to change and come back in time. There isn't any time to stop and think at the strangeness of this request. She rushes home and is back in due time, donning a black chiffon sari with the wispiest silver lining, the sheerest diamond earrings, Aldo heels and wrapped up in her favourite Chanel perfume. The car stops in front of the office where she is surprised to find Nagesh waiting for her along with his new found friend. Since he is the host Nagesh steers the man to the back seat while he sits down in the front. Pallavi who has been dreaming of the most passionate reunion with her man, feels extremely cheated at this turn of events. For her the evening is already ruined before it could take off.

Nagesh introduces his guest as Mr. Narender Suri the sole distributor of their competitive brand in Chandigarh and Punjab. It seems he is the uncrowned electronics king with important underworld connections. For the last six years he, with all his legal, illegal muscle power, had been ruling the roost in that region, which also happened to be the largest electronics market among all states of India. Nagesh said, "For the last five years, I've been desperately trying to woo dear Mr. Suri. Finally his daughter married the son of our distributor in Gujarat and I struck lucky." This provoked another bellow of full throated laughter from the man sitting uncomfortably close to her, displaying his beetle stained teeth so brazenly. Mr. Suri had a pan masala tin which he kept offering to Pallavi much to her distaste.

The dinner is a pathetic affair, with Nagesh pouring out drink after drink, Mr. Suri totally inebriated, Nagesh looking tipsy, having had one too many for company, their voices getting louder and louder and their talks more vulgar. It is so impossible for her to believe this side of the suave, gentle Nagesh; but Pallavi knows his single minded focus, his burning ambition to raze the competition altogether and therefore can see through his desperation. Dinner over they sit out in the open coffee shop in the gardens. Mr. Suri by now has completely loosened up and makes every effort to lean over her, touch her and make personal remarks which infuriate her no end. Since he is the guest, she dare not be rude, but the situation is becoming absolutely unbearable. She tries to catch Nagesh's eyes, a number of times, but he chooses to overlook it. She just can't believe this is happening to her.

Over coffee Mr. Suri announces his desire to see their manufacturing plant in Chennai. Nagesh is most willing to arrange for it and while they are working out the details for a two day visit, Mr. Suri pipes in, "Mr. Krishnan with your permission, I would like to have Ms. Pallavi as my guide. Make our tour for next Thursday and Friday, so that we can spend the weekend together and maybe she can show me a bit of Chennai too. After all, a man needs to relax also, doesn't he?"

Pallavi is stunned to say the least. She can't believe she has heard what she did. She feels the blood draining away from her face, her heart pounding out loud, palms moist, hoping that the earth would open up and swallow her right there, right then. Oh, the sheer temerity of this shameless sleazy man. She feels so humiliated and defiled by the very sound of his proposal and turns to her man, confident that he'd give it back to him good and proper. Nagesh who cherishes her as his own, who holds her as his only love of life, knowing fully well that he has been and shall forever be the only man for her.

But to her horror, she sees him smiling his usual charming smile and saying, "Well, why not Mr. Suri. Your desire is our command today and always. You have asked and it shall be done."

Pallavi sits back as if in a trance and stays so till Nagesh bids adieu to Mr. Suri at the hotel. In the car neither of them speaks a word. Once home she begs him to come up for a minute. As he walks in, she closes the door and without a word falls on his chest sobbing and crying, "Oh, how could you do this to me Nagesh? How could you expose me to such a lech? How could your blood not boil when he made such a disgusting demand? Why did you not kill him there and then?"

He allows the outburst to take its course then disengaging himself slowly, quips, "Oh, come on Pallavi, cut it out, will you? That's the problem with you women; you all talk of emancipation, empowerment but are not ready to pay the price for it.

"OK, so we both fell for each other, it has been a wonderful affair, no regrets; but that does not make you my wife, does it? Don't get possessive on me. I'm here to look after my interest and so are you. It's quits really.

"Why should I be annoyed with Mr. Suri? Who doesn't like to spend a weekend with an attractive woman? All of us do that, in different places, at different times, without any guilt. He just lacks class and style, but he's powerful and that is a far more attractive quality in a man. If I were you, I'd drop everything and go and enjoy it too. It'll go down in your favour, trust me. Sleep on it baby and tell me tomorrow."

He turns around and leaves without a backward glance. Pallavi stares at the closed doors, long after the sounds of footsteps have died out. Much later when the realisation hits her, she drags herself into her bedroom and falls down on the bed weeping uncontrollably.

She weeps for all her dreams that have crashed right in front of her today like a pack of cards falling in a heap.

She weeps for that love which was her ultimate tribute to the man who she thought had all the values she revered. Little she did know that she was running after a mirage.

She weeps for all her ideals in life which she couldn't save despite every effort. She weeps for all her strife and struggle that she had gone through every day of her life to create an identity for herself.

She weeps for the desire to be an equal human being, transcending all limitations of gender, to earn her dignity and pride in life.

All her life she thought she was cutting her shackles which hampered her freedom and her flight. But she realises now that be it Vidhi or Maya or Pallavi, be it Kakori, Allahabad, Mumbai or Delhi; a woman carries her chains inside her all her life and from womb to womb through generations.

Her tears totally spent, she sat down in deep contemplation. Well, she thought, so she had failed. So what? When the challenges are phenomenal, failures are bound to be there. It was not her failure as much as it was the failure of the man and his society. The chains were not so much her chains, as it were theirs, binding them down to their mental handicap. The more she thought of it, the stronger her resolve grew. She would not be a quitter. She would get up again and fight. She would cut those shackles again and again and yet again, till they become hollow and weak and fall apart on their own.

She walks up to the other room and peeps inside. Her eyes fall on Maya, deep in her sleep, a half smile paying on her innocent face. Her heart warms up to her. Yes, this is where she would start her journey this time round. Building up the broken strength of this young helpless girl, giving her the confidence to face the world, giving her the power of knowledge, helping her to spread her wings and fly above and finally being the wind beneath those wings.

✦ ✦ ✦